...words and words alone can capture and convey the full awareness of a living mind.
—Dr. Benjmain Dunlap

My favorite thing about this discipline is that there is no rule that isn't a dare.
—Drew Johnson

The novel...always wriggles out of the rules thrown around it.
—James Wood

...writing a novel is about the limitlessness of your imagination.
—Adriana Trigiani

I am a firm adherent of what Wright Morris said...how do I know what I want to say until I've said it?
—Thomas E. Kennedy

Sometimes the language of the story is the story.
—Sam Lipsyte

You can do anything, as long as you do it beautifully.
—Ellen Akins

You have to travel some roads you don't know. You have to learn to play again...
—Renée Ashley

It is essential for a writer not to be afraid of his mind.
—Thomas E. Kennedy

NO RULE THAT ISN'T A DARE:
HOW WRITERS CONNECT WITH READERS

Essay and Interviews

by

Bill Mesce, Jr.

Serving House Books

No Rule That Isn't a Dare: How Writers Connect with Readers

ISBN: 978-0-9971010-2-7

Cover photograph by Tsung-Lin Wu from 123rf.com

Serving House Books logo by Barry Lereng Wilmont

Published by Serving House Books, LLC
Copenhagen, Denmark and Florham Park, NJ

www.servinghousebooks.com

Member of the Independent Book Publishers Association

First Serving House Books Edition 2016

To everyone who has ever sat at the keyboard praying
for the next word to come.

"Writing is easy;
all you do is sit staring at the blank sheet of paper
until the drops of blood form on your forehead."
—Gene Fowler

BOOKS BY BILL MESCE, JR.

FICTION:

The Advocate (w/ Steven G. Szilagyi)
Officer of the Court
The Defender
Precis: A Collection of Short Stories and the novella "Diamond Red"
A Cold and Distant Place

NONFICTION:

*Peckinpah's Women: A Re-Appraisal of the Portrayal of Women in
    the Period Westerns of Sam Peckinpah*
*Artists on the Art of Survival: Observations on Frustration,
    Perspiration and Inspiration for the Young Artist*
Overkill: The Rise and Fall of Thriller Cinema
*Reel Change: The Changing Nature of Hollywood, Hollywood
    Movies, and the People Who Go to See Them*
*Inside the Rise of HBO: A Personal History of the Company that
    Transformed Television*
*Idols, Icons, and Illusions: The Movies We Love – and Love to Hate – and
    the People Who Made Them.*

CONTENTS

INTRODUCTION 9

ON "SHOW, DON'T TELL"—"WHAT DO YOU MEAN YOU CAN'T DO IT?" 14

FICTION: ELEGANT JUGGLER—Adriana Trigiani and *The Shoemaker's Wife* 33

PERIOD FICTION: THE DEVIL IS IN THE DETAILS—Steve Szilagyi and *Photographing Fairies* 39

WAR STORY: WAR AMONG THE RUINS—David L. Robbins and *War of the Rats* 44

HARDBOILED FICTION: THE CASE OF THE DISAPPEARING PRIVATE EYE—An Interview with Ariel S. Winter 50

CRIME FICTION: A GOLDEN EAR—George V. Higgins and *The Friends of Eddie Coyle* 56

ROMAN NOIR: RAISING CAIN—Charles Ardai on James M. Cain's *The Cocktail Waitress* 60

WAR STORY: BEEN THERE, DONE THAT—Richard Herman and *The Peacemaker* 68

MEMOIR: BEING HIS OWN PUNCHLINE--Bill Persky and *My Life Is a Situation Comedy* 73

MEMOIR/CRITICAL ANALYSIS: A LIFE REFLECTED IN

ART; THE ART REFLECTED IN A LIFE—Kier-la Janisse and *House of Psychotic Women* 78

TRUE CRIME: AN INSIDE JOB—Sonny Grosso, Philip Rosenberg and *Point Blank* 84

TRUE CRIME: COP'S EYES—Adam Plantinga and *400 Things Cops Know* 89

PULP FICTION: PRESERVING AN ICON—Max Allan Collins on Mickey Spillane 97

GENRE INVERSION: BLACK AND BLUE—Thomas E. Kennedy and His Non-Noir Noir, *Beneath the Neon Egg* 105

WRITERS ON WRITING: A WRITER'S REBOOT 113

CONTRIBUTORS 151

REFERENCED WORKS 163

ACKNOWLEDGMENTS 165

INTRODUCTION

Before sitting down to write this introduction, I did an Amazon search for books about writing. There were 54,483 results.

You can cull that herd down by being more specific. Search for books about fiction writing: 1,483. Nonfiction: 1,358. Unless you're famous, there seems to be little interest in your memoirs which would explain why the results for books on how to write your memoirs number a (comparatively) paltry 341.

Even taking into account a fair percentage of duplicate results, those are some hefty numbers; even the 341. It's a reasonable question to ask, then, if the world needs another book on writing. Or, let me put it another way: what's left to be said? Fair question.

Speaking in extremely broad generalizations, many if not most of these books seem to fall into one of three broadly generalized categories:

1) The how-to's. These are books like Nathan Bransford's *How to Write a Novel: 47 Rules for Writing a Stupendously Awesome Novel That You Will Love Forever,* and Randy Ingermanson's *How to Write a Novel Using the Snowflake Method,* and – of course – *Writing Fiction for Dummies,* by Ingermanson again and Peter Economy. The typical conceit in these books is that there's some sort of formula (or formulae), template, system, etc. (Bransford's 47 rules; Ingermanson's Snowflake Method – "Ten battle-tested steps to jump-start your creativity" according to the Amazon description) which can take the aspirant from blank page to commercially viable manuscript.

2) It's art. A more high-minded approach views the writer as artist, writing as art, and the driving impulse an amalgam of personal expression and personal philosophy. I'm thinking here, looking at my own personal bookshelf, of John Gardner's *On Moral Fiction:* "Art begins in a wound...and is an attempt to learn to live with the wound or to heal it." Or James Wood's

How Fiction Works, in which every example is drawn from the top ranks of fine literature.

3) Counsel from a star author. Stephen King's *On Writing.* Here, the commercially successful author explains their own process, with the idea (sometimes implied, sometimes overtly stated) that what-worked-for-me-should-work-for-you.

To one degree or another, in one respect or another (determined by the nature and needs of the reader), these are all of value. And, they are all valid, at least in my view, even if they are, at least at times, in conflict with each other.

Concerning that validity, well, remember the old saw, "Even a broken clock is right twice a day"? All writers are different; different sensibilities, different tastes, different ways of working, etc. For some, the discipline of "Write 10 pages every day" is the structure they need. For others, it's a ball-and-chain that turns a creative pleasure into a tedious chore. Some like the steps of outline, note cards, working out bios for each character, while others simply spill their created stuff out onto the page and discover their story and characters in the rewrite process.

And therein is the shared weakness in these books, all across the three categories: they rarely acknowledge that difference; that what might work perfectly well for this writer over here, can be a route to frustration and despair for that writer over there. I'll go one step further: a system or methodology that works for a writer beautifully on one work may be utterly useless on another.

Let me offer an example from my early screenwriting years (not to equate screenwriting with crafting prose, but it's also a fun story about the insanity of Hollywood and the hubris of young writers).

I was in my late 20s, and it was my second professional outing. I had been contracted to do an adaptation of a bestselling novel. I had, by that time, done a lot of reading about screenwriting, particularly William Goldman's *Adventures in the Screen Trade* (still, to my mind, the best book about writing for the screen because instead of offering a system, Goldman takes you through the often different processes of problem-solving for each of his projects). I went into this adaptation gig with a system in mind based on what I'd read: strip the book down to its narrative spine – its essentials – then rebuild a screen story around that spine. From the accounts of Goldman and other veteran screenwriters, I had also learned that producers and studio development executives feel compelled to mess with your stuff. One screenwriting trick was to deliberately include stuff you knew was unnecessary, and then when the non-writers started futzing with your work, you would horse trade, offering to cut the fat you'd built in so you could keep your treasured cuts of meat. The problem that my readings hadn't prepared me for: my people wanted to keep the fat and cut the meat.

Still, this system of stripping down a novel's narrative had worked well enough in the main that I was feeling a bit cocky when I was offered another adaptation job. "Ok," I thought, "I know how to do this now." Except the novel I was hired to adapt didn't have a narrative spine. The chapters were almost stand-alones, and the book developed no forward momentum until the last chapter or two. The system I had used on the previous gig was useless. There was nothing to strip down; a narrative and character arcs had to be created from scratch, and then incidents from the novel woven into this newly-manufactured structure.

Now I grant, writing a movie, which jams a lot of cooks into the kitchen – from studio "creative executives" to the guy from the marketing department – is a different animal from prose, but the concept that what works on one project doesn't necessarily work for another isn't. It took ten drafts, over 150 rejections, and immersing myself in the work of John LeCarre to find the first person voice for my first novel, *The Advocate*, in a cynically philosophical, good-with-words Scottish reporter. But in my novella *Diamond Red*, the first person narrator is a possibly dying, delirious, hardly-a-writer combat soldier. In opposition to the carefully composed architecture of *The Advocate* and its fluid, polished style, *Diamond Red*'s story pinballs between three time lines and is told in the terse, tough style of someone who doesn't write for a living.

Point being you don't write *The Old Man and the Sea* the same way you write *Jaws*.

In my late 50s, with ten books and some screenplays and works for the stage under my belt, I went back to school, entering the Creative

Writing MFA program at Fairleigh Dickinson University. One of the first things that pushed a button for me was a clear articulation of a vague feeling I'd been stumbling my way to over thirty-odd years of writing: that there are no rules, there is no one-size-fits-all system. Every writer is different; every writer's brain works a different way, their goals are different, their goals in individual works are different. Learning to write is, in large measure, an exercise in self-discovery: figuring out how *you* work so you can figure out what system (if any, and one of your own devising) works for you.

The other crucial concept I picked up on in the MFA program – and, not to back-pat myself too much, but also another idea I'd been realizing on my own – was that one cannot be *taught* to write; one *learns* to write, and one learns by studying how other writers do things (LeCarre "taught" me how to style *The Advocate)*.

The major tool to develop this skill – and reading to learn how to write is a skill in itself – is the "close reading." In this, the student studies a particular aspect of a creative work, analyzing it, breaking it apart, trying to figure out the how's and why's behind an author's choices, tactics, and strategies.

Because I had been kicking around for some time before I'd come into the program, I had the advantage over other students of knowing some writers. In my close readings, I didn't have to guess or make assumptions; I could ask an author to explain his/her thinking.

In this process it became evident to me that an often overlooked aspect of the craft of writing is that it is often about problem-solving: Adriana Trigiani figuring out a way to design the parallel narratives making up most of her bestseller, *The Shoemaker's Wife;* Max Allan Collins trying to immerse himself in the voice of Mickey Spillane so he could finish Spillane's uncompleted final works.

Collected here, then, are those analytical readings in which I was able to involve the writer (or a credible authority on the work i.e. Nicholas Pileggi on the work of crime fiction maestro George V. Higgins, and editor Charles Ardai on *roman noiriste* James M. Cain's posthumous last novel) directly in a discussion on the strategies and tactics applied to a particular work. Hopefully, in this body of pieces, the aspiring writer sees an overarching concept: that each author finds his/her own way, and that each work presents its own distinct challenges.

Bookending these analytical pieces are two essays. The first is an in-depth examination of one of the most tossed-around canards in the how-to circles of writing: "Show, don't tell." My hope here is that the reader, like myself, learns the only rule in writing is there are no rules.

The collection ends with a piece which takes the reader through the experience of my first residency at the Fairleigh Dickinson MFA program. My hope here is that the reader realizes, as I did, that a writer is never too old or too experienced to learn new things. Perhaps also there are some lessons to take from the bumps and detours of one writer's journey. There is also the council and observations offered from a host of established writers participating in the program as mentors and visiting lecturers ranging from poets to novelists, non-fiction writers and those involved in the tricky business of literary translation.

As human beings, we think visually, yet to express ourselves on the page we are restricted to the inexact universe of words on a page. Writers are at war with the limitations of the written word, and it is a war without a Geneva Convention. When it comes to trying to connect with a reader, to make the reader see what we see and feel what we feel, we have to be ruthless in our willingness to go around, cheat, bend, and break the rules.

Our victory is a reader who turns the last page sorry that it is the last page, and who settles back in his/her chair with a satisfied sigh wanting more.

ON "SHOW, DON'T TELL"
"WHAT DO YOU MEAN
YOU CAN'T DO IT?"

Long ago in my undergraduate years, I hit a block in a manuscript I was working on. I went to Dave Wesner, the graduate assistant in my Creativity Class, a very sharp guy more accessible than the professor he was assisting.

When I described my problem, Dave's head reared back: "What do you mean you *can't* do it?"

"You're not supposed to do it."

"What's that mean: 'not *supposed* to'? Why not? Says who?"

"It's, like, a rule."

"Rule?" For a second there, Dave sounded like Sessue Hayakawa in *The Bridge on the River Kwai* ("You speak to me of *rules?"*). "There's no rules, Bill. There's only *one* rule: 'Whatever Works'."

Whenever I hear something that amounts to a writing rule – whether tacit, implied, suggested, or overtly proclaimed – Dave Wesner *a la* Sessue Hayakawa comes back to me: "You speak to me of *rules?"*

Maybe it's because of my own long, combative experience with it, but I get particularly agitated when I hear the rule, "Show, don't tell."

Simplicity – three little words; it doesn't get much simpler — however, does not automatically bring with it clarity. Depending on who's doing the bromiding and who's doing the rebutting, you'll find there can be some argument over what constitutes showing and what constitutes telling. What's usually meant is a preference for the concrete over the abstract; for what can be seen rather than contemplated; for prose that is descriptive and physical action that defines character and/or drives the plot over the lyrical, the introspective, the reflective. Literary critic Wayne C. Booth (1921-2005), in his *The Rhetoric of Fiction*

(1961), describes "telling" as the author revealing to the reader what no "real life" observer could possibly know. Writer Francine Prose, in her *Reading Like a Writer: A Guide for People Who Love Books and for Those Who Want to Write Them* (2006), describes the concept more bluntly: "...don't tell us a character is happy, show us how she screams 'yay' and jumps up and down for joy." I don't know if I'd go as far as novelist Joshua Henkin who, in an article on writersdigest.com entitled, "Why 'Show, Don't Tell' Is the Great Lie of Writing Workshops," declares:

> ... 'Show, don't tell' is...an implicit compact between a lazy
> teacher and a lazy student when the writer needs to dig deeper
> to figure out what isn't working in his story.

But I will say that considering the aesthetic dynamics of the printed word, when it applies to strong writers (and that's the caveat: *strong* writers writing *strongly*), the line between showing and telling is always in play, and sometimes even disappears completely as showing and telling merge into a single, powerful instrument. Nick Carraway tells the story of *The Great Gatsby*, but his narrative consists primarily of showing. Literature is filled with passages and even entire novels which, says Francine Prose:

> ...(contradict) a form of bad advice often given young writers –
> namely that the job of the author is to show, not tell. Needless to
> say, many great novelists combine "dramatic" showing with long
> sections of the flat-out authorial narration that is, I guess, what
> is meant by telling. And the warning against telling leads to
> a confusion that causes novice writers to think that everything
> should be acted out...when in fact the responsibility of showing
> should be assumed by the energetic and specific use of language.

In the end, the distinction between the two, depending on the dexterity of the author, may be meaningless. As the author Ellen Akins is fond of telling her writing students, "You can do *anything*...as long as you do it beautifully."

•

I wrote my first professional screenplay in 1979, and made it through the next dozen years without once hearing anything on subsequent jobs even approximating "Show, don't tell." But by the 1990s, I was finding a creeping change in the lexicon of screenplay development. There were a lot more references to "story/character arcs," "beats," "three-act structure," and – you guessed it – "Show me; don't tell me" (sometimes punctuated with a condescending, "There's a reason they call them *movies*, Bill").

I peg the change as starting in the 1980s. Robert McKee began his now-famous STORY seminars in 1983 (adapted into book form 14 years later as *Story: Substance, Structure, Style and the Principles of Screenwriting*). Not long after, Syd Field wrote his first of several books on screenwriting, *Screenplay: The Foundations of Screenwriting; A Step-by-Step Guide from Concept to Finished Script* (1984). Those two books – which, in the '80s/'90s, seemed to rapidly become the accepted bibles of the trade among a rising young cohort of screenwriters, agents, and production people – opened the door to a flood of how-to-write-a-successful-movie tomes (a recent search on Amazon for "screenwriting books" turned up almost 3600 results). The idea behind most of these books, from what I can see, is that there's a formula or template that, if followed, produces an effective screenplay. If you insert Tab A into Slot A, you wind up with a movie as good as *The Godfather* or *Chinatown*.

By the time I started getting hit with "Show, don't tell" as a screenwriter, I had already had enough experience under my belt to know that, as an overriding cinematic aesthetic, it was more or less bullshit. The "Show, don't tell" people may have the writing gurus on their side (Field doesn't even get out of his Introduction before defining a screenplay as "...a story told with pictures"). I have Aristotle.

In his book *Aristotle's Poetics for Screenwriters: Storytelling Secrets from the Greatest Mind in Western Civilization* (2002), one-time Miramax story analyst Michael Tierno, inspired by Aristotle's *Poetics*, rates "spectacle" – in Aristotelian terms, the physical elements of production – as the *least* important element of drama coming behind, in descending order of importance, plot, character, character thought, dialogue, and music. The art of visual spectacle belongs to the set designer; the art of drama to the poet.

The justification for "Show, don't tell" as a screenwriting axiom *seems* obvious; movies are a visual medium. You're forced to work with only what you can show. What shoots holes in the concept is that in the decades before people who didn't write movies started writing books telling people how to write movies, there were any number of films that did more telling than showing (or showed characters doing more telling than doing).

Take that classic early *noir, The Maltese Falcon* (1941). John Huston's screenplay is nearly scene-for-scene, line-for-line taken from the 1930 Dashiell Hammett (1894-1961) novel. For the most part, the movie, like the book, is nothing more than scenes of exposition and explanation. Its characters do little more than talk and talk and talk, including about a number of key events that happened off-screen. The aesthetic of *Falcon*, with only a few tiny exceptions, is that of "Tell, don't show."

In the film's "climax" (I use quotes because, like most of the movie, *Falcon*'s cathartic moment is still *more* talk), *Falcon* demonstrates the cinema's frequent *need* to go interior – to get at the turmoil going on inside a character – and does so through that hoariest of dramatic devices: the revealing monologue. Humphrey Bogart's private eye Sam Spade feels compelled to explain at length to *femme fatale* Bridget O'Shaughnessy (Mary Astor) why he's "sending her over" to the cops for killing his partner, even though he's in love with her and didn't seem to care much for his colleague. But Bogie's soliloquy (which is even longer in the novel) is as much there to provide a window for the audience into his bruised and roiling soul as it is an explanation for desperate, uncomprehending Bridget:

> Listen. This won't do any good. You'll never understand me but I'll try once and then give it up. When a man's partner is killed, you're supposed to do something about it. It doesn't matter what you thought of him, he was your partner and you're supposed to do something about it. And it happens we're in the detective business. Well, when one of your organization gets killed, it's bad business to let the killer get away with it. Bad all around, bad for every detective everywhere...I've no earthly reason to think I can trust you, and if I do this and get away with it you'll have something on me you can use whenever you want to. Since I've got something on you, I couldn't be sure you wouldn't put a hole

in me some day. All those are on one side. Maybe some
of them are unimportant; I won't argue about that. But
look at the number of them. And what have we got on the
other side? All we've got is maybe you love me, and maybe
I love you...maybe I do. I'll have some rotten nights after
I've sent you over but that'll pass. If all I've said doesn't
mean anything to you, then forget it and we'll make it
just this: I won't because all of me wants to regardless of
consequences, and because you counted on that with me the
same as you counted on it with all the others...

Stephen Whitty, film critic for *The Star-Ledger*, offers a more recent example of telling playing better than showing:

> *In Jaws (1977)...(the character of shark hunter) Quint remembers a time in World War II when his ship sank and sharks circled the stranded sailors. As visual a filmmaker as (director Steven) Spielberg is, he resists the urge to give us a flashback and show us the bloody water, the hungry fish, the screaming men. Instead, he just lets Quint tell us – and makes <u>us</u> fill in the horrible details. What we imagine is far more horrible than anything he could show.*

Quint's quite lengthy monologue – which doesn't exist in the source novel – not only explains his Ahab-like obsession with shark-killing, but gives his ball-busting hardass character a tragic, even sympathetic underpinning the action of the movie cannot provide.

"If you think of films often cited as 'perfect' movies," says Stephen Whitty, "whether it's old Hollywood films like *Casablanca* (1942) or more modern classics like *Chinatown* (1974) – it's not just the pictures you remember. It's the characters' voices."

There are entire film genres which are dependent on telling: stage adaptations, mysteries with reams of exposition ("The killer is here in this room!"), courtroom dramas ("You can't handle the truth!"). When I hear "Show, don't tell" in connection with screenwriting, one of the first titles my mind goes to is *12 Angry Men* (1957), Reginald Rose's big screen adaptation of his live TV drama. *12 Angry Men* not only depends on telling, it's *about* telling, with the dozen titular jurors grappling with iffy testimony about off-screen events as they stumble toward what they think might be the truth of a murder case. The only thing we're shown are people arguing about what they've been told.

Across genres, for one reason or another, various filmmakers – sometimes even those considered the most visual of directors – have drawn on devices dating back 2500 years to the days of Hellenic theater because there are limitations to showing; showing can't always get us inside a character, or inside a character's story. Pumped for an opinion, teacher and stage director Dr. Suzanne Trauth, author of several books on theater and one-time head of the B.F.A. in acting program at Montclair State University, says:

> Though "telling" might be an unappreciated word now, there is a long tradition of "story-telling" as a mode of engaging....Where the visual isn't as blatant...someone had better do some telling to set the scene...

These "telling" devices include self-revelatory soliloquies (like the *Maltese Falcon* and *Jaws* examples above) and any variety of voiceover approaches often operating as another form of soliloquy and/or cinema's version of a Greek chorus. Says Stephen Whitty, "The device encourages us to see the events through these (characters') eyes, to take their point of view...Words seduce us in ways images never could." Martin Sheen's hushed, first person voiceover in *Apocalypse Now* (1979) gives Francis Ford Coppola's Vietnam epic a narrative cohesion and tonal underpinning the story on the screen doesn't always have ("It's a way we had over here for living with ourselves. We cut 'em in half with a machine gun and give 'em a Band-Aid"); in *Raising Arizona* (1987), Nicolas Cage's low-key narration keeps the movie's screwball express train montage sequences from flying apart, and also provides a certain soulfulness to the rapid fire comedy ("Sometimes it's a hard world for little things," juxtaposed with the Biker of the Apocalypse blowing up a desert hare); in *Little Big Man* (1970) and *Barry Lyndon* (1975), voiceover narrations are even more true to the nature of an ancient chorus, offering both editorial commentary and a bit of historical context along with a peek into characters' interior workings (from *Barry Lyndon*'s omniscient narrator: "No lad who has liberty for the first time, and twenty guineas in his pocket, is very sad, and Barry rode towards Dublin thinking not so much of the kind mother left alone, and of the home behind him, but of tomorrow, and all the wonders it would bring"). The comic Westerns *Cat Ballou* (1965) and *Waterhole #3* (1967) have a literal chorus; troubadours (an on-screen Stubby Kaye and Nat King Cole in *Ballou;* an off-screen Roger Miller in *Waterhole)* who sing narrative bridges, flashes of character insight, and even a bit of frontier philosophizing (from Miller: "The code of the West is to do unto others...before they do it unto you").

Even a cinematic *maestro* like Alfred Hitchcock found himself hitting the wall on showing, struck by the need to find some way into a character's interior in a scene in his classic *Vertigo* (1958). Kim Novak presents herself to private eye James Stewart wearing an outfit which makes her look exactly like a woman Stewart was in love with and who died in a previous case gone wrong. Stewart forcefully takes her in his arms and crushes his lips to hers. But the visual message – at least according to Steven Spielberg's regular composer, John Williams — is incomplete.

In a TCM special on movie music, Williams used the clip as an example of movie music telling us something that's not on the screen. Without Bernard Hermann's swelling, swirling score, says Williams, not much is happening in the scene. But the music reflects i.e. tells of the emotional turmoil churning away inside Stewart.

I offer up, in summation, writer/director Ron Shelton's refutation of a younger generation of filmmakers' blind allegiance to "Show, don't tell." "(The) old canard that action defines character is only partly true," Shelton argued in an interview. "Hamlet wasn't doing a whole lot when he said, 'To be or not to be.'"

If "Show, don't tell" is hardly ironclad for a visual medium, what weight should it carry for prose? After all, whether you show it or tell it, in prose, the bottom-line fact is it's still words on a page.

•

Google around the Internet to find the literary roots of "Show, don't tell," and what comes up quite often is Ernest Hemingway's (1899-1961) "Iceberg Theory," also referred to as the "theory of omission":

If a writer of prose knows enough of what he is writing about he may omit things that he knows and the reader, if the writer is writing truly enough, will have a feeling of those things as strongly as though the writer had stated them. The dignity of movement of an ice-berg is due to only one-eighth of it being above water.

From *Death in the Afternoon (1932)*

But the roots of the concept go back even further. Anton Chekov (1860-1904), who died when Hemingway was only five years old, had his own take on showing instead of telling. In an 1886 letter to his brother Alexander, Chekov wrote:

When describing nature, a writer should seize upon small details, arranging them so that the reader will see an image in his mind after he closes his eyes. For instance: you will capture the truth of a moonlit night if you'll write that a gleam like starlight shone from the pieces of a broken bottle, and then the dark, plump shadow of a dog or wolf appeared. You will bring life to nature only if you don't shrink from similes that liken its activities to those of humankind.

Descriptive, narrative-driven *showing* kind of storytelling goes back further still. In his book, *How Fiction Works* (2008), literary critic James Wood dates the beginning of the realist narrative tradition to Gustave Flaubert (1821-1880), but we can go back beyond that: millennia, in fact. Look at *Beowulf* (which may date to the 8th Century), *The Iliad* (8th Century B.C.), the books of the Old Testament some of which are at least as old:

It happened, late one afternoon, when David arose from his couch and was walking upon the roof of the king's house, that he saw from the roof a woman bathing; and the woman was very beautiful. And David sent and inquired about the woman. And one said, "Is not this Bathshe'ba, the daughter of Eli'am, the wife of Uri'ah the Hittite?" So David sent messengers, and took her; and she came to him, and he lay with her.

From *Second Book of Samuel*

All of these narratives relate a series of physical actions with very few interior insights; they *show*. David sees Bathsheba, he gets a case of the hot and hornies, he boinks her.

But even in some of the earliest forms of story-making, story-makers recognized the limits of showing; they knew there was something else going on, some pivotal interior drama that could not be rendered in imagery or action (Aristotle's "character thought"). The ancient Greeks used the vehicle of a chorus to tip off the audience to back story, subtexts and meanings, and unseen ramifications of what they saw playing out on stage. From Sophocles' *Oedipus Rex* (c. 429 B.C.): "'Twere better sleeping ills to leave at rest." Or, in plain English, "Hey, Oedipus, I'd leave this alone if I was you!"

Leap ahead a few thousand years and we see a literary movement developing focused on exploring this other, unseen, psychologically interior realm. We see precursors in Chekov, which, you have to admit, is kind of ironic since he was the guy with that moonlight on the piece of glass business. But Chekov is more famous for stories in which not a lot happens on the surface; there's not a lot to *see*. He was writing stories propelled not by action, but by the mullings and musings of his characters.

Similarly, Henry James (1843-1916) was writing fairly dense stuff not because his stories don't have a lot happening, but because what happens is deeply wedded to what's going on inside his characters. *The Turn of the Screw* (1898) is as much in its narrator's head as it is on the maybe/maybe not haunted grounds of the estate where she's governess to two children. It's probably no coincidence, then, that it was James' philosopher/psychologist brother William who came up with the label for the signature style of the literary form evolving toward the latter part of his brother's career: "stream of consciousness."

The Modernist movement, inspired by the theories of the world's most famous shrink, Sigmund Freud, saw a new, vastly under-explored terrain in the interior landscapes of the mind. What was going on *inside* characters was, at the very least, as important as what they were doing.

The author who is usually marked as the launch pad for the modernists was Marcel Proust (1871-1922), and probably nobody stretched the idea of going deep (telling) instead of going forward (showing) as much as he did. In his magnum opus, *In Search of Lost Time* (published over the span 1913-1927), the work's signature moment comes early in the first volume, *Swann's Way*:

> ...one day in winter, as   came home, my mother, seeing that I was cold, offered me some tea, a thing I did not ordinarily take. I declined at first, and then, for no particular reason, changed my mind. She sent out for one of those short, plump little cakes called 'petites madeleines', which look as though they had been moulded in the fluted scallop of a pilgrim's shell. And soon, mechanically, weary after a dull day with the prospect of a depressing morrow, I raised to my lips a spoonful of the tea in which I had soaked a morsel of the cake. No sooner had the warm liquid, and the crumbs with it, touched my palate than a shudder ran through my whole body, and I stopped, intent upon the extraordinary changes that were taking place. *(Charles Kenneth Scott-Moncrieff translation)*

That extraordinary thing is a flood of memories of the narrator's childhood years in the village of Combray which constitute 148 pages of free-flowing, plotless recollections of both images and sensations.

Granted, within *Lost Time* there's a fair amount of showing over the course of seven volumes, but since these are memories, as with any memory, one recollection tumbles into another without any moving the plot – when there is one — forward. Each memory is like a fireworks detonation, bursting free of its container and ranging in glowing wiggles across the page, digression compounded by digression. Herewith one of the narrator's seemingly random Combray memories:

> It was in these 'Month of Mary' services that I can remember having first fallen in love with hawthorn-blossom. The hawthorn was not merely in the church, for there, holy ground as it was, we had all of us a right of entry; but, arranged upon the altar itself, inseparable from the mysteries in whose celebration it was playing a part, it thrust in among the tapers and the sacred vessels its rows of branches, tied to one another horizontally in a stiff, festal scheme of decoration; and they were made more lovely still by the scalloped outline

of the dark leaves, over which were scattered in profusion, as over a bridal train, little clusters of buds of a dazzling whiteness.

The description of hawthorns goes on for another one-third of a page for no apparent purpose other than to illustrate the vividness of the memory to the narrator. Much of *Lost Time* reads similarly. In the eyes of author/academic Dr. Benjamin Dunlap:

> *Proust is as verbal as great art can be, but I vividly see, hear, and feel all the great scenes of* In Search of Lost Time. *And yet, it's his language in those long ruminative passages that is the most distinctive aspect of his greatness, the ways in which, I'm inclined to argue, words and words alone can capture and convey the full awareness of a living mind. He does show us many things...But his magic resides unforgettably in the words...*

The goal of the modernists was to mimic the non-linear, chaotic pinballing of human thought. Virginia Woolf (1882-1941), another prominent figure in modernist literature, in her 1919 essay, "Modern Novels," codified the philosophy of the modernist work thusly:

> *...there would be no plot, little probability, and a vague general confusion in which the clear-cut features of the tragic, the comic, the passionate, and the lyrical were dissolved beyond the possibility of separate recognition.*

An example of Woolf practicing what she preached herewith from her 1931 novel, *The Waves:*

> "I see a ring," said Bernard, "hanging above me. It quivers and hangs in a loop of light."
> "I see a slab of pale yellow," said Susan, "spreading away until it meets a purple stripe."
> "I hear a sound," said Rhoda, "cheep, chirp; cheep, chirp; going up and down."
> "I see a globe," said Neville, "hanging down in a drop against the enormous flanks of some hill."
> "I see a crimson tassel," said Jinny, "twisted with gold threads."

Despite the quotation marks and our assumption that the characters are talking to each other, this isn't really dialogue, the characters are not together, and what we are reading is an impressionistic mosaic of thoughts from connected but geographically distant characters. The novel follows this group of long-time associates through much of their lives, and is told throughout in this oblique style of non-dialogue representing the thinking – sometimes topical, sometimes reflective – of its characters.

Arguably, no one pushed the modernist aesthetic further than James Joyce (1882-1941), particularly in his novel *Ulysses* (1922), and especially during the book's final chapter and the section known as "Molly Bloom's Soliloquy." It is a densely written, stream-of-consciousness passage which, despite its length, consists of only eight sentences including what's considered the longest sentence in English literature coming in at almost 4400 words. To the casual reader, this torrent of verbiage may seem chaotic, but it is sculpted chaos — to steal a phrase from contemporary author/essayist Thomas E. Kennedy, "artful artlessness" – in which there really is design and purpose and crafted flow. The modernists who, like Proust and Joyce, skated closest to the edge, present something on the page akin to those optical illusion prints which offer what seems a meaningless visual pattern, but in which, as you stare deeply and long enough, one can eventually discern a distinct image.

If we put modernism in its most extreme Joycean form at one end of the curve, and the "Iceberg Theory" at the other, we find the bulk of the curve falls in between with authors who saw the value of wedding showing and telling. Consider William Faulkner's (1897-1962) novella, "The Bear" (1942). While the bulk of the story about the annual pursuit of a local legend – a marauding bear – is told in a generally descriptive manner, once the bear is killed (a highly symbolic act in the piece), the story vaults into a stream-of-consciousness passage contemplating the larger meaning of the bear's death; a passage which includes another Joyce-like syntactical monster, an 1800 word sentence taking this bit of reflection to a psychological peak.

According to Stephen Whitty:

The reason that novelists like Faulkner and Joyce are so tough to film is that nobody ever read those writers for their plotting; you read them for the words, for the ideas, and if you only concentrate on the storytelling, as movies tend to do, you lose a great deal of what makes them work. The eternal power of The Great Gatsby *comes from the words on that last page, as Fitzgerald talks about America, and hope, and romanticism and dreams; he uses the green light at the end of Daisy's pier as a symbol, but for a filmmaker to just show us that light without the words accompanying it is to strip the image of its meaning.*

Most contemporary authors, including those of literary caliber, seem to see showing and telling as the yin and yang that, together, comprise a narrative whole. John Barth's *The Floating Opera* (1956) has a clearly discernible plot: narrator Todd Andrews writes about the day he decided to commit suicide (and obviously didn't). Yet the novel slides easily between past, present, and into numerous introspective digressions and psychological doodlings which have nothing to do with the plot, and are often neither showing nor telling but reflective pauses in the forward movement of the book. These side trips may not qualify as stream-of-consciousness, but they're cousins to the concept. Look at the novel's first chapter – "Tuning My Piano" – a "meandering stream" (the narrator's words) of thoughts from this non-writer about his sitting down to write this story. "No doubt when I get the hang of storytelling, after a chapter or two," writes Andrews, "I'll go faster and digress less often"; Tom Kennedy's "artful artlessness."

Another example, this from Gish Jen's *World and Town* (2011). Unlike Barth, Gen writes in a leaner style: simpler vocabulary, simpler syntax. But she, too, moves easily between the exterior and interior of her characters — between showing and telling — as one of her main characters reflects on her day-to-day existence as she spends time sitting at an easel outside her home, paintbrush in hand:

Hattie's no artist. Joe used to call her Miss Combustible, and probably in her day she was indeed lit more by the blindness of the world than its beauty. Vietnam! Staff firings! Library closings! She fought them all. But her chief job these days is to reconstitute herself. *(That you might rise and fight again,* Lee would say – one of her favorite quotes being from some old warrior who is said to have said, as he lay a-drip on a field, *I'll but lie and bleed awhile. Then I will rise and fight again!)*

The passage continues on for quite some time – over a page in length – before the novel begins to move forward again. Throughout the novel, Hattie does not always manifest what's going on inside her through her actions. She's a ruminative woman carrying the weight of a fair bit of personal history, all of which we get through Jen's telling us about them. As the novel's point of view moves from one character to another, Gish gives them all their similarly reflective interior moments. "(Fiction)," writes Joshua Henkin, "can give us thought: It *can* tell" (my italics).

The push-pull between showing and telling isn't reserved for higher literary circles. It makes sense that showing dominates telling in mainstream commercial fiction since most readers – I'm supposing, here, but it seems a reasonable supposing – prefer to "see" people get punched out, things get blown up, and glowy vampires run off and elope with sullen teen girls. That's visceral; of course that's a more fun read.

Yet a number of significant commercial fiction writers excelled at using telling as their vehicle of choice. Remember *The Maltese Falcon?* Hammett's novel is a first-person narrative, Sam Spade telling us this story about people telling each other about things that happened that we never see. Consider that monologue we looked at earlier. What we have is the narrator, private eye Sam Spade, telling us about his telling Bridget O'Shaughnessy why he's ratting her out to the cops. That's as much a telling as telling gets.

One of my personal favorites is Edgar-winning author Ross Thomas (1926-1995) whose crime novels – think of *The Sting* with a noirish edge – often feature recurring characters. With their typically byzantine plots tied to fairly detailed back stories, large chunks of Hammett-like expository dialogue are common:

> "Floyd Ranshaw, the singing cop – wasn't that what they called him?"

"He wasn't bad, either," she said. "Not good, not bad. He sang his way through college, club dates, weddings, what have you and then joined the cops in Pelican Bay and became the youngest lieutenant in its history – the padrone of the East Side. It's almost pure ghetto over there, you know. Part black, part Chicano, part poor white. And he knew them all. Or a lot of them, anyhow, and they liked him because he was honest and fair..."

From *Chinamen's Chance* (1978)

And so the speaker's portrait of Ranshaw goes on for almost a half-page. But without it, Ranshaw who appears only infrequently in the novel (a regular trait of Thomas' novels are large casts of supporting characters floating in and out of the main plot), would be close to a dramatic zero if readers are reduced only to what they can see of him.

In commercial fiction, few authors have taken this strategy of telling over showing as far as crime fiction author George V. Higgins (1939 – 1999). A one-time Massachusetts district attorney, Higgins – according to true crime author and screenwriter Nicholas Pileggi – used wiretap recordings of real-life hoods as the model for his dialogue. In the Introduction to the Picador edition of Higgins' first and arguably best novel, *The Friends of Eddie Coyle* (1970), another noted author of crime novels, Dennis Lehane, writes:

Ah, the dialogue. It takes up a good eighty percent of the novel, and you wouldn't mind if it took up the full hundred...Open any page of this book and you will find vast riches of the spoken word. The characters here love to talk; they'd probably talk to a chair...In most novels, talk is the salt and plot is the meal. In The Friends of Eddie Coyle, *the talk is the meal. It's also the plot, the characters, the action, the whole shebang.*

Most of Coyle's dialogue has little or nothing to do with the novel's plot. It's often elliptical, digressive, typically going the long way around to make a point which, in itself, may be irrelevant. For instance: Dillon, a police informant, meets with his contact, the conversation wanders, Dillon mentions a man who came into the bar he owns carrying a porn magazine which leads to mention of a friend who owns an adult bookstore which leads to:

"I got a strong notion you couldn't put my friend outa business with anything short of a bomb, you know? I know this guy about six years now, I never see him take a bust. I never see him in any kind of trouble, he's always got a few dollars on him, dresses fucking respectable, always got a shirt and tie on, and I think this is probably about the ninth thing he's been doing. He hadda a bar for a while, then he was doing something in show business, I see him last year at the track, he's got a nice Cadillac."

All told, this digression about the "friend" who never appears in the book and is completely irrelevant to the proceedings takes up nearly two full pages after which the conversation only then crabwalks into the point of the meet. Again, Dr. Benjmain Dunlap:

...to quote Walter Pater (and) his observation that "all arts constantly aspire to the condition of music"... Music neither shows in a visual sense nor tells in a verbal sense, but it communicates powerfully and coherently.

Higgins pushes his dialogue to the level of music; what is being said is unimportant. Higgins delights in the sound of the words, the rhythms, the very meaninglessness of the exchanges. As author Sam Lipsyte told a 2013 Fairleigh Dickinson MFA residency, "Sometimes the language of the story is the story," and Higgins' is always all about the language of the story.

In ironic contrast, Higgins' prose is so lean he makes Hemingway look blabby. Eddie Coyle – the connecting thread holding the novel's various criss-crossing plotlines together – is introduced on the first page simply as "The stocky man," with never another physical detail offered throughout the novel. His character comes to us in what he does, but even more so through what he says and how he says it.

Coyle's streams of dialogue bring up the notion that sometimes telling is showing. The argument can be made, and it has been, that all this pointless, foul, shapeless dialogue in *Eddie Coyle* is actually showing us something; the pointless, foul, shapeless lives the novel's characters lead.

Emphasizing the point, look at this passage from Joseph Conrad's (1857-1924) 1896 short story, "The Lagoon":

> For the last three miles of its course the wandering, hesitating river, as if enticed irresistibly by the freedom of an open horizon, flows straight into the sea, flows straight to the east - to the east that harbors both light and darkness. Astern of the boat the repeated call of some bird, a cry discordant and feeble, skipped along over the smooth water and lost itself, before it could reach the other shore, in the breathless silence of the world.

"The Lagoon," on the one hand, follows Chekov's dictum about what it takes to bring a setting to life. But on the other, this is less descriptive than it is about conveying not an image, but a sense of the place. I would argue this constitutes both showing and telling; communicating the power of a visual through language more poetic than descriptive.

This isn't just how-many-angels-can-dance-on-the-head-of-a-pin semantic debate. There's a practical craft aspect at stake here. That the line between showing and telling can be blurred in this manner – one might even argue the dividing line is purely subjective and therefore arbitrary – only reinforces the idea that "Show, don't tell" reads better than it plays, right up there with "Always bet a horse with four white socks," and it's good luck when a bird craps on you. The very concept of there being a "do" and a "don't" risks channeling writers still learning their trade down a path where they're more worried about violating rules then finding their way to tell a story in the way the nature of that story demands (the misstep Dave Wesner so righteously got on my case about forty years ago). "It is a mistake to regard a certain stereotyped structure as the inviolable essence of the novel," says Czech writer Milan Kundera in his *The Art of the Novel*.

Let's take this thought a step further and consider that the reason the line between showing and telling blurs so easily is because when it comes to the written word, the concepts are meaningless.

The page "shows" us nothing because there are no images for us to see. Whether we are being shown or told, we have only the printed word. The writer's task is to provide textual cues in the hope of triggering in the mind of the reader images and sensations stored in the reader's mental data bank. It's a form of connect-the-dots, with a writer's prose providing the dots and the reader having to make the connections. The more deft the writer is in the placement of the dots, the stronger the response of the reader, and there is nothing in the annals of literature or psychology that I'm aware of guaranteeing a stronger reader response through descriptive prose than in aiming for something more interior. James Wood offers the notion that "...Flaubert and his successors (give) the sense that the ideal of writing is a procession of strung details, a necklace of noticing, and that this is sometimes an obstruction to seeing, not an aid." And from Joshua Henkin:

> *If you ask me, the real reason people choose to show rather than tell is that it's so much easier to write "the big brown torn vinyl couch" than it is to describe internal emotional states without resorting to canned and sentimental language. You will never be told you're cheesy if you describe a couch, but you might very well be told you're cheesy if you try to describe loneliness. The phrase "Show, don't tell," then, provides cover for writers who don't want to do what's hardest (but most crucial) in fiction.* (Henkin's parentheses.)

•

I differ with Joshua Henkin in that I think "Show, don't tell" is a perfectly fine tactic. It lends an elegantly simple brutality to Cormac McCarthy's *Blood Meridian* (1985) the same way it grants an elemental simplicity to Hemingway's *The Old Man and the Sea* (1951). It's the perfect vehicle for those stories. But "Show, don't tell" is only a tool; not *the* tool, no better or worse than any other tool in the writer's kit. Says Milan Kundera, "Ironic essay, novelistic narrative, autobiographical fragment, historic fact, flight of fantasy: The synthetic power of the novel is capable of combining everything into a unified whole like the voices of polyphonic music." "My favorite thing about this discipline," commentator Drew Johnson told his friend, author Matt Bell, on Faulkner choosing to tell some sections of *The Sound and the Fury* rather than show, "is that there's no rule that isn't a dare."

The use of "Show, don't tell," or any other writer's tool, shouldn't be based on some writing guru's edict, but on the writer's choice that this is the best, most appropriate way of telling a given story. Proust would've drowned Hemingway's *Old Man*: "Every time he smelled the salt air, he saw the sea in all the colors he'd ever seen in it season by season, year by year; emerald green, royal blue, aquamarine, topaz, azure, sapphire, Elizabeth-Taylor's-eyes violet..." By the same token, Hemingway would've destroyed the delicious ambiguity of *The Turn of the Screw*: "Maybe I saw a ghost. Maybe I didn't. It was time to put the kids to bed."

"The novel," says James Wood, "is the great virtuoso of exceptionalism: it always wriggles out of the rules thrown around it." Our energy, as writers, shouldn't be to worry – with Dave Wesner's warning always ringing in my ears – about what we're supposed to do/not do, but in developing the expertise to applying all the tools available to us, all the colors on the palette, all the strategies and tactics our cunning can devise to tell a story in a way that makes a reader go, "Holy crap!" or sniffle, or grin a little, in a way that is neither cheap nor exploitative; to "...do it beautifully." Anybody can make a guy gasp by kicking him in the nuts; the good writer gets the same reaction without pulling on verbal Doc Martins.

Since I have yet to develop a full command of my own toolbox, I'm going to give the last words to the man I consider my first creative mentor, Benjamin "Bernie" Dunlap:

> *(Proust's) magic resides unforgettably in the words – proving what? That every medium the mind might seize upon can be used to this same end – movement, colors, wood or marble, even smoke signals I suppose. No single formula, not even what I've just said about language, can ever contain the human imagination, which, when all has been said, sung, and shown, may well be the message towards which all art continually aspires.*

FICTION:
ELEGANT JUGGLER
Adriana Trigiani and
The Shoemaker's Wife

It's no great secret that there are popular authors – some who are *immensely* popular – that are not particularly good writers. Their success is more dependent on their ability to find a sweet spot in the audience and hit it effectively than it is in their command of language and literary craftsmanship. By the same token, there are truly powerful writers – literary class talents – who don't find or who have some aim other than hitting the sweet spot. And then there are those who have a foot in each camp; who can entertain a mass audience, but do so through a strong command of the writer's craft. Adriana Trigiani is one such writer, and one of the best examples of her craftsmanship is in the elegant structure of her 10th novel, *The Shoemaker's Wife*.

An epic romance inspired by stories of Trigiani's grandparents, *The Shoemaker's Wife* is the story of Ciro, given up as a young boy to a convent by his widowed and destitute mother, and Enza, product of a somewhat less desperate but nevertheless impoverished family living not far from where the nuns are raising free-spirited Ciro and his more devout brother Eduardo. The story sweeps from the beautiful but poverty-plagued Italian Alps of the early 1900s, to the teeming immigrant neighborhoods of turn-of-the-century New York and New Jersey, to the American Midwest, spanning nearly four decades in the process. For over 300 pages of the 470 page novel, Trigiani sets her characters on a tarantella, whirling about each other, their paths intersecting only occasionally, sometimes only glancing, enough so to generate a welcome sense of doubt; that perhaps the story of Ciro and Enza is one of what-could-have-been rather than romantic inevitability.

According to Trigiani:

> *When you have two protagonists, you almost have to outline their arcs as though there are two separate novels. Then, you take those arcs, and using a timeline, weave the two storylines together. [The two stories end] up to be equal because if the writer takes the time in the outline stage, he or she can see where the two lives intersect for maximum effect. Also writing this way helps you see where one life needs to rise up in the story to meet the other, then blend them.*

In fact, outlining has become more important to Trigiani, and *The Shoemaker's Wife* amply demonstrates why:

> *More and more, I outline – I arc, I shape and I think about the order of things. It helps a lot because you have to keep the entirety of the piece in your head as you work, and the more you can check your outline, the better. It just helps you the writer to know the road, and, of course, you can always change it, but (the outline) gives you parameters – a level of security.*
>
> *When intersecting storylines, the tension of the narrative comes from the push and pull of the desires and needs of those characters, sometimes for one another, sometimes for a higher purpose, like winning a war, sometimes for a noble cause like making enough money to buy the family a house, but there is something driving them towards one another...I just try to keep the story moving, and keep the characters moving towards one another.*

The novel opens with 10-year-old Ciro and his older brother Eduardo being left at a convent by their mother, with Enza – also 10, and living in a nearby village — not being introduced until page 15. It will be another 57 pages (and six years in the novel's chronology) before Ciro and Enza meet for the first time when he is employed to dig the grave for Enza's young sister, felled by a blood disease. Trigiani explains how this intersection works not just as the characters' introduction to each other, but as a foreshadowing:

The idea that the two young lovers meet in such a tragic
way forebodes their own eventual sad ending [Ciro dies
prematurely], but it also defines their mission as a couple. They
will be one another's salvation and strength and reprieve and
balm, no matter what comes. He will do the heavy lifting, and
she will abide with him. She will be steadfast and he will be
faithful. It's a painful tableau to witness as a reader, but you
don't forget it.

When Enza's father allows her to drive Ciro back to his
village, it is she who takes the reins of the horse and drives
him home in the carriage. One of the most beautiful and
unsettling images to me is when he returns to his foster home
inside the convent and she steers the horse and carriage back up
the mountain alone in the dark. Ultimately, this is what will
happen to her at the end of their life together; she will have to be
strong and face life without him. On that ride home, as a young
girl, she is almost deciding if the pain is going to be worth it.

Of course, you read the next 400 pages and decide for
yourself. The intersections come, and then they are separated by
these lily pads where the character, alone, figures out what just
happened and plots a course for himself or herself. I like those
potent moments.

By the time the burial episode ends, each is etched in the mind
of the other, but then Ciro is sent to the U.S. to avoid the wrath of a
priest whom he's discovered in a flagrante delicto with one of the local
girls. While Ciro works in America as a shoemaker's apprentice, the
situation of Enza's family becomes more financially precarious, and
she and her father travel to America in the hopes of making enough
money to support the family back home. Ciro happens to be in lower
Manhattan's St. Vincent's Hospital being treated for an injury when
he's asked to translate for a recent arrival made deathly ill by her trans-
Atlantic passage. The woman is, of course, Enza.

For another 160 pages or so, Trigiani manages to keep the dance
going in similar fashion. Sometimes the two meet, the sparks rekindle,
but chance separates them. Other times, they just miss each other

either figuratively (Enza tracks down Ciro to the shoemaker's shop where he works only to find that, having lost track of Enza, he has involved himself with another woman), or literally (Ciro, now at liberty, tracks Enza to the house in Hoboken where she'd been living only to find she's moved away).

And so it goes, the pages otherwise filled with other relationships (including Enza's near-marriage to another man) and experiences reflecting, in miniature, the great turn-of-the-century Italian immigration, ascendance, and eventual assimilation, until the two – now mature adults – finally connect:

> Ciro took Enza's face in his hands. "I have loved you all my life. I was a boy who knew nothing, but when I met you, somehow I understood everything...I know I disappointed you when I didn't come for you, but it wasn't because I didn't love you, it's because I didn't know it yet."

And then, from Enza, the long-awaited response:

> "I belong to you, Ciro," she said.

Some of these points of intersection were sparked by real-life events Trigiani discovered in doing the historical research required to bring the period and locations to three-dimensional life:

> *I always find the gems in the research. The places where the characters meet one another come from some random event I find buried in the newspaper or in an obituary, or even casually mentioned in an unpublished diary. These finds set me off in a direction with an idea.*
>
> *One of my favorites is the night that Enza and Ciro meet at the opera before Ciro sets off to fight in World War I. Enrico Caruso did a few fundraising concerts for the war, and that got me to thinking: wouldn't it be wonderful if, in a sea of doughboys in uniform, Ciro spots Enza in a lovely gown?*
>
> *I had a true story from my grandparents. My grandmother was walking home from the factory in Hoboken when she heard the Bergamosque dialect spoken in the chatter on the street corner. She turned to look and saw my grandfather in uniform speaking with another soldier. It was the first time she laid eyes*

on him. From there they had a conversation. They wrote letters
back and forth from France. I fictionalized those days, of course,
but the essence was true.

Whether one responds to the sentimentality and romanticism of *The Shoemaker's Wife* is, of course, a subjective matter, but less subjective is the careful construction of these two often separate but just as often teasingly close plotlines. It's reasonable to assume Trigiani gained at least some of her dexterity for disciplined structure from the early part of her career when she wrote for television in the 1990s. By nature of set running times and commercial breaks, TV shows enforce a rigid, inflexible story template.

Trigiani's particular writing routine also offers a lesson in how "... to keep the entirety of the piece in your head..." In a 2008 interview posted on the website for West Virginia Public Broadcasting, Trigiani described her daily process when she sat down for hours of work:

I always read in from page one. I don't start on page 42 where I left off last night...And then when I read in I create the new material.

For the writer attempting a sprawling, multi-threaded narrative, each narrative line a universe in itself with its own cast of characters and arc, *The Shoemaker's Wife* is an accessible demonstration in how to keep so many balls in the air in smooth trajectory. And should that story, like Trigiani's, be based on some bit of personal history, she charges the writer not to be restricted by the facts:

I imagine events and moments (in The Shoemaker's Wife*) – why not? It's a novel, not a biography.*
Furthermore, it's the craft of novel-writing to encompass a world, to take in the entirety of that world and celebrate it, a time and place, the people of that time and place, their music, style of dress, politics, their fears – all of it. I love that about writing novels. The truth is really at the heart of the emotions; everything else is framing. I think you can stray to your heart's delight.
The idea here is to be free; writing a novel is about the

limitlessness of your imagination. It's about putting people in rooms and situations and places and times together that they might not normally ever be, including jumping centuries if that's the writer's inclination. Play with the form.

The key is the word itself: "novel." Be novel – original, new, fresh, untried. Have at it.

PERIOD FICTION:
THE DEVIL IS IN THE DETAILS
Steve Szilagyi and
Photographing Fairies

A period piece with ambitions beyond the visceral appeal of, "And then he ripped her tight bodice from her heaving bosom," faces challenges both obvious and subtle. Those hurdles need to be addressed in a layered strategy beginning with the foundation of a piece (which may be partly or even totally invisible), reaching through obvious gross descriptive elements to those most minute i.e. a small, innocuous physical detail, a bit of obscure arcanum, a precisely chosen word. The endgame is to produce a work neither superficial nor one that feels calculatingly researched, but lived-in, organic, whole — *authentic*. For period works told in the first person, the challenge multiplies since now the author also needs to find a voice appropriate to the period, aiming for a balance between linguistic accuracy and accessibility. Author Steve Szilagyi puts on an expert how-to display of period writing in *Photographing Fairies*, a fantasy drama set in post-WW I England loosely based on the 1917 affair of the Cottingley Fairies.

Szilagyi's choice of the postwar period is neither arbitrary nor superficial, but strategic necessity in his story of American expatriate photographer Charles Castle chasing down a wild tale of fairies in a small rural village. According to the author:

> *The choice of period is inseparable from the content of the story. The mid-1920s was a time of disillusionment. The Great War had destroyed many people's ability to believe in God or the constituted authorities. Arthur Conan Doyle (a key character in the novel) had created a great modernist character in Sherlock Holmes: an unsentimental scientist–policeman who trusted no*

one and took nothing on faith…But as G.K. Chesterton once said, "People who don't believe in God don't believe in nothing. They believe in <u>anything</u>."

Szilagyi does not belabor this point in the novel, but integrates it through occasional fleeting – but direct — touches. "It is London," narrates Castle in the novel's opening pages, "In this nervous, third decade of the twentieth century. These giddy years after the Great War." Still later, when the caustic, doubting Castle leaves a meeting with Doyle, himself obsessed with his own bizarre spiritualistic pursuits, Doyle's words echo in Castle's mind:

> We are at a crossroads in history…Mankind has just emerged from a great and terrible war. The current peace is violent and vexing. The next war will be more horrifying than the last. And the war after that – it is difficult to contemplate."

Doyle's spiritualism is fact-based. Along with him, the rest of Szilagyi's characters are also searching for something to fill their respective disillusion-created spiritual voids. As Doyle's daughter explains, "The world is changing…A new worldview is opening up…," then amplifying with "…today the field of religion is crowded with competing sects, all claiming to be true, and all appearing – to intelligent people at least – to be ridiculous," a sentiment aptly capturing both the spiritual hunger and its desperate nature which characterized the period.

Those are the broad parameters of Szilagyi's story, set on the bedrock of the historical spiritual upheaval of the 1920s, making his story both true to its time, and of its time. To tell that story, Szilagyi adopts an arch, formal style which gives the book a faintly, properly archaic feel (he describes it as "…a kind of combination Robert Louis Stevenson and P.G. Wodehouse"). He avoids the florid prose often associated with vintage works, generally keeping his language and syntax clear and simple, occasionally flavoring it with a bit of Old Lit vocabulary; a balance between a period-appropriate style and accessibility for the contemporary audience. One of the best examples is a passage where Castle, Proust-like, flashes back to a sensation he had as a child in Boston:

> I recall the approach of midnight when I was a child. Lying
> in my bed, in my little room over my father's North End shop,
> trembling beneath a quilt lovingly sewn by a grandmother's
> hands, I would stiffen as the Old North Church chimed the
> quarter hours after eleven; the hands of its black-faced clock
> inexorably crawling toward "the witching hour" (a phrase
> heard once, and destined to echo forever between my ears).
> How to hold in abeyance the terror emanating from midnight
> and all its implications?

As for the details which bring the world of that story to life, Szilagyi advises:

> *The period details are many but <u>not obvious</u>...* (emphasis
> mine). *The most important period work in historical fiction...is
> what you don't put in. You have to know a great deal about the
> period in order to avoid anachronisms such as technology that
> has not yet been invented, words and phrases that were not in
> use, references to historical events that had not yet happened or
> were not widely known, etc. There is a whole 'tone' to a period
> that you have to capture...(which) calls for the author to be
> saturated in research and prior knowledge of the period and its
> cultural products.*

In other words, the author needs to be so deeply immersed in the vocabulary, attitudes, period phrasing, the small day-to-day details of the period that they come as naturally to his/her writing as they do to the characters in his story, while, at the same time, the author must resist the urge to showboat his/her research.

In the same reflective passage cited above, Castle remembers the sounds of "ordinary life" – that ordinary life being one lived during the closing years of the 19th Century — going on outside his boyhood bedroom window:

> ...the clop of a passing cart horse; the laughs of late-night
> revelers; distant train whistles; the wheels of the rubbish cart
> grinding against the paving stones.

There's a similar passage, this one in the narrator's contemporaneous London, as he walks the great old city's streets:

41

> I strolled hither and yon, down thoroughfares wide and
> narrow. Passed parks, palaces, and hovels; plunged into the
> City. Around me, humanity surged like a pitching sea; black-
> frocked financiers muttered in doorways; peddlers howled;
> locomotives thundered. I saw a one-legged veteran begging
> in the Strand. I passed a jeweler's where a turbaned Indian
> was buying a glittering brooch.

Still earlier in the novel, Castle walks along those same avenues with the country constable – Walsmear — who has come to him with a bizarre story about fairies:

> The thoroughfare was giving forth its usual midday
> cacophony...You could distinguish street vendors, taxicab
> horns, gear-grinding omnibuses, and the shrieks of the street
> arabs.

At other times, Szilagyi maintains the illusion of period with a well-chosen, precisely placed word or phrase:

> "Constable Walsmear, I wonder if I might **stand you to lunch**"
> (emphasis mine)

> Strolling **hands-a-pocket** through crowds...

> It was Walsmear. He was dressed in full constable's **fig**, with
> badge, helmet, and blue coat.

> "Your friend...Constable Walsmear. He was driving the
> **motorcar.**"

> He was dressed in white shorts and a white **singlet**.

And then, of course, there are those delightfully precise physical details, such as the older woman whose life is saved from a mugger by her out-of-date whalebone undergarment: "The malign intent of Shorty's blade had been deflected by a sturdy corset." Castle's description of Linda Drain, a minister's wife with whom Castle falls in love, is informed by Szilagyi's careful study of fashion of the day: "She was wearing an ink-blue chemise, with a pattern of small, dark triangles, and a flounce that stopped just below her silk-stockinged knees. A smooth white cap with a little point on the crown clung to her head like an inverted buttercup...she lifted her cap and smoothed the crinkly, bobbed hair beneath."

With Castle's occupation that of photographer, Szilagyi needed "...to get the types of camera and darkroom equipment used in the 1920s down to the last detail, or the book would just be stupid..." He was lucky enough to find a how-to book from the time of the events in the novel at the General Society of Mechanics and Tradesman's Library, and his research provided him with one of the novel's most memorable dramatic coups.

Linda Drain visits Castle as he works in an ad hoc darkroom set up in a country church cellar. According to Szilagyi:

> *In the chapter on darkroom technique, I came across some astonishing advice... The "how to" book advised amateur photographers to take off their clothes before going into the darkroom, and cover their bodies with (mineral) oil to keep dust or skin flakes from falling onto the developing film or plates.*

Castles warns Linda away, cautioning her from the dark that he is naked and covered in oil.

> (From Linda) "Are you afraid that I've brought dust into the room?
> "It's not your fault. But you probably have. Unless – "
> "Yes?"
> "Unless you've taken off your clothes and covered yourself with mineral oil. Ha ha."
> "But I have."

Unsurprisingly, working closely together in the dark, feeling the heat of their respective bodies, one thing leads to another, and their heretofore repressed passion consummates itself, all thanks to Szilagyi's discovery of this forgotten bit of period-appropriate ancient photographic technique.

It is the deft application of all these elements – large and small, by turns exercised in depth or mentioned in passing – which convincingly transport the *Photographing Fairies* reader to a time and place long gone, but, for the moment, alive again on the page.

WAR STORY:
WAR AMONG THE RUINS:
David L. Robbins and
War of the Rats

Countless novels have been written about World War II, so many one wonders if there could possibly be stories left to tell. From gritty realism (Harry Brown's *A Walk in the Sun)* to literary grandeur (Norman Mailer's *The Naked and the Dead)* to black comic absurdity (Joseph Heller's *Catch-22)* and surreal allegory (William Eastlake's *Castle Keep)*, WWII lit seems a wide, deep canon in which the stories worth telling have already been told and retold...and retold.

And yet...

The breadth of the greatest armed conflict in history remains under-appreciated; to a younger generation for whom WW II is as relevant as the War of 1812, maybe even forgotten. It touched, directly or indirectly, every continent. It was fought in farmlands and cities, on arctic tundra, in sweating jungles and blistering deserts. It was fought on land, in the air, at sea, even under the sea. Somewhere between 50-60 million human beings were killed (the majority of them civilians) between the historical start of the war in September of 1939 and its atomic climax in August 1945. To give you some idea of the scope of the loss: that's as if every human being in the American northeast – from Pennsylvania to the Atlantic, from New Jersey to the Canadian border – was killed.

In the U.S., the war touched everyone...literally. Over 15 million men and women served in the American military, and several hundred thousand more in attached civilian organizations (like the merchant marine). That means approximately one out of every nine Americans served during the war (contrast that today where the ratio is less than one in one hundred including those serving in the National Guard and reserves).

In other words, the number of stories about the war is infinite, the only limitations being that of imagination, and, perhaps more importantly (and sadly so), marketability.

Beginning in 1999 with *War of the Rats*, David L. Robbins turned out a string of bestselling novels about World War II that focused on the overlooked, the undersung, and the plainly forgotten. Most of these novels, either in part or *en toto*, deal with the war in the east where Germany and the Soviet Union were locked in a death struggle of fantastic proportions. While we in the west think of the war in Europe through our own defining moments – D-Day, for example, or the Battle of the Bulge – the fact is that even the largest engagements on the western front were dwarfed by the apocalyptic fights in the east. The Battle of Kursk (the basis for Robbins' *Last Citadel)* stands as the largest tank battle in history, the armored duels of both Iraq wars paling in comparison. Similarly, the violence of the fighting staggers the imagination, with the invading Germans brutalizing the peoples of the east whom they viewed as subhuman, and the Soviet troops, in turn, inflicting a horrific revenge as they pulverized their way into Germany (the fall of Berlin to the Russians comprises the final act of Robbins' *The End of War)*.

War of the Rats is set against the Battle of Stalingrad (the title is a translation of *rattenkrieg* – the German soldiers' nickname for the fight): a six-month slugging match in 1942 which became nothing less than a contest of wills between Hitler and Stalin (the city itself was of no great strategic value). But harkening back to the philosophy of journalist Ed Murrow – that one tells the big story by telling the little story – *Rats* focuses on a one-on-one duel between two ace snipers: Sergeant Vasily Zaitsev of the Soviet Army, and Colonel Heinz Thorvald of the German SS.

The contrast between the two is the Battle of Stalingrad – in fact, the war in the east – writ in miniature. Zaitsev is peasant stock, taught to hunt by his grandfather not for sport but to put meat in the pot. Although his marksman's expertise has made him an unwilling pawn in the Soviet Army's socialism-salted propaganda, Zaitsev, the common man, fights because he has to; for his comrades, for survival, to repel the invader.

Thorvald, on the other hand, is an officer, aristocratic, arrogant, specifically assigned by the German high command to score their own propaganda victory by killing Zaitsev. Thorvald, master of Germany's sniper school, learned to hunt as a gentleman's sport, and he stalks Zaitsev in much the same frame of mind, devoid of either patriotic fervor or loyalty to his brothers-in-arms, but simply to out-ace another ace.

Making the story even more compelling is that Robbins' narrative is a dramatization of a true story. In that, Robbins had to deal with the questions faced by any author of historical fiction: what are the boundaries? How far can history be stretched? When does dramatization compromise the integrity of the tale?

Robbins discusses the writing of *War of the Rats:*

War of the Rats *is based on an actual historical event. How much research did you have to do, and how obligated did you feel to get the history right?*

Historical fiction calls on all the writer's knowledge of the heart and mind required of any well-told story: love, hate, jealousy, fear, sorrow, the panoply of emotions and motivations that make up a human. That's a big enough challenge for any storyteller. For historical fiction, you also have to load up an *intimate* understanding of the context for the tale: the gone times, places, machinery, sentiments, culture, and, in my case, weaponry, the workings of two great militaries, the actual record of mass events (Stalingrad!). Then, just when you know everything you've set out to learn, after you have all your Gullivers staked to the beach, you must combine the two: the mercurial human and the immensity of history. Nothing short of this effort will make a compelling narrative out of the materials of the past.

As far as feeling obligated to getting the story right because it actually happened, I prefer to be guided by profound truths as well as real ones. This means I follow those events, actual or made-up, which best express the story I'm trying to tell. First priority is to mine the truth, to find those factual events and people I deem dramatic enough to be included.

Once that's exhausted, I invent only those scenes and characters that can carry the banner of the tale *authentically*. Seamlessness is what I look for. A reader shouldn't be able to parse between the real and the pretended.

You interviewed the real Vasily Zaitsev, as I recall. How much of a difference did it make to have spoken with one of the actual participants? Were you concerned that this asset might give the character in the novel a weight you might not be able to give Heinz Thorvald or the other characters?

The real Zaitsev was very old, quite sick when we spoke, but very willing to talk about his adventures in Stalingrad. It's always an irreplaceable gift to speak with an actual participant of the events in your book. The responsibility you mention of overweighting one character beyond another actually worked the other way: it pressed me to pay even more attention to the flesh and bones and makeup of the antagonist Thorvald, to make him a fully measured match for Zaitsev.

While the novel is based on real events and you are using real characters, this is still obviously a dramatization. To what extent did you feel obligated to remain within the facts of this duel? Did this feel like a constraint? Did you ever feel, "Who's going to know?" Did you, at any point in the book, "cheat" the history to take the story to a given place?

I did, in fact, "cheat" the history. I gave in to my publisher's wish that there be an American character in the book, and so gave Tania Chernova, in real life a young woman from Minsk, the background of a woman caught in the German attack on the city while visiting relatives, who then becomes a feared sniper (and thus got back on track with her true arc). I will never, ever, do that again. The story didn't require it: the business did. They are not the same, and business shares few interests with writing.

Beyond that obvious act, I stayed true to the facts as the records and survivors, among them Vasha Zaitsev himself, related them. I would have diverted, and without conscience, had the real events not been sufficiently driving. But, it turned out they were, and I had a real playground of history. The key, I believe, is to choose well; then, this issue of changing the story doesn't come up so much.

You maintain, for much of the novel, parallel narratives. Was there any plan to that construction, or did it develop organically? Was balance a concern?

The novel is a duel, and paralleling the points of view seemed a natural structure. It fit the back and forth of the drawn-out confrontation, and, just as importantly, granted the reader access to facts that the other character in the duel lacked. This is the essence of tension, asymmetrical information.

This is a fight during World War II on the eastern front about which I think most Americans know little. Was there a concern that readers might be so in the dark about the context of this fight that you'd lose them?

I suppose there might have been, but as a young and avid writer, I didn't let myself think of anything but the story. I explored the human parts of it very well, I think, the love between Tania and Vasha, the grudging respect between the antagonist snipers, the loyalty and fervor to both cause and country of the troops who made Stalingrad such a killing ground. The result of not thinking about the possibility of a confused or disengaged audience allowed me to focus on the universalities of the story, seeing my characters not as Russian or German but in wider, more recognizable human roles, just frightened, fearsome, lonely men and women. And that, more than anything, made the book successful, I believe.

Did you get a chance to walk the ground? Obviously, Stalingrad has long since been rebuilt, but did it make a difference to your writing?

Absolutely. I have never depicted any major setting in any of my books that I have not personally visited. Stalingrad , Poland, the Russian steppe, the South African bush, the Saudi desert, Manila, Sydney, the list is growing as I will be heading for Viet Nam this summer. You must go to your locations, for you will see that which you could never, truly never, have guessed. A gargantuan sunflower field outside Prokhorovka in Ukraine, the pillars of crashing water against the Malecon in Havana, the carcasses of rhinos butchered for their horns in the Kruger National Park, the savagery of Stalingrad preserved in several square blocks of the city left unrestored. Writers, go. Go.

HARDBOILED FICTION:
THE CASE OF THE DISAPPEARING PRIVATE EYE
An Interview with
Ariel S. Winter

I looked for him, but he was gone. I checked the boozy dives and the greasy spoons and the street corners where the not-nice girls hang out.

Nothing.

He was gone.

Tall guy, fedora, trench coat. You must've seen him. Usually smoking. He was always hanging around, poking his nose where it didn't belong and usually getting it punched.

A real wisenheimer, too, always cracking wise.

You see him, you call. And if I find out you've been holding back...

If you don't miss that kind of patois, you're either too young to remember it, or you've got a tin ear. God knows, *I* miss it.

As it happens, I've recently read an advance copy of Ariel S. Winter's bravely ambitious debut novel, *The Twenty-Year Death*, which Titan Books is releasing this month. Audaciously constructed, *The Twenty-Year Death* is actually three stand-alone mystery novels which combine to tell a greater, overarching story of violence and tragedy. Set in three different decades – the 1930s, 1940s, and 1950s – each echoes popular crime fiction from its time: *The Dain Curse*-type mystery for the 1930s, the hard-boiled patter of Sam Spade for the 1940s, and the angst and cynicism of *noir* in the 1950s. Winter's assured command of each suggests a writer at home with much of the private eye canon (unsurprising, I guess, from a long-time bookseller), and a good guy to ask about what happened – and what's happening – to the private eye genre in print...

In print, the private eye story dates at least to Edgar Allan Poe's Auguste Dupin stories in the 1840s. The genre seems to connect with American audiences in a truly American way with writers like Dashiell Hammett and Raymond Chandler in the first half of the 20th Century. How do you see the evolution of the private eye story? What was it about the genre that engaged you?

The evolution of the private eye story proceeds from detectives in the 19th and early 20th Centuries like Dupin and Sherlock Holmes who prize deductive reasoning over action, to in-the-thick-of-the-action detectives like Sam Spade and Philip Marlowe in the 1930s and 1940s. The Marlowe model then dominates the next several decades, with the only significant development the introduction of the female private eye like Sara Paretsky's V. I. Warshawski, and Sue Grafton's Kinsey Milhone in the 1980s. These women, however, were still modeled on the hardboiled detectives of the pulp era. All of these detectives follow a strict moral code, whether that moral code coincides with the law or not. Then, in recent years, there's been something of a subversion or appropriation of the private detective in books like *Motherless Brooklyn* by Jonathan Lethem, *Look at Me* by Jenifer Egan, and *Inherent Vice* by Thomas Pynchon where the detective is flawed, and his code of honor is looser.

I would also argue that bounty hunters and superheroes often function like private detectives, so if you're looking at current film, I wouldn't discount the Batman — he is the world's greatest detective after all — or Tarantino's upcoming movie, *Django Unchained*. And, of course, there's the popular BBC show *Sherlock*, the Robert Downey, Jr. Sherlock Holmes movies, and another network Sherlock Holmes show about to start. Obviously, Holmes is a special subset on his own, but he is a private eye.

As to what attracted me to the genre, I'd probably say the attitude. My favorite movie as a child (and possibly still today) was *Who Framed Roger Rabbit?* (1988), which is a gateway movie in that it has the cartoons to draw a kid in, but it is solidly a hardboiled detective movie. Around the same time, I began reading Paretsky and Grafton, and shortly after that I became a diehard comic book fan, especially *Batman*, so the lone, grim detective was something I've always liked. I like their fearlessness, their strong moral code, their steadfast determination.

The glory days for the private eye story, in both print and film, seem to be from the 1930s into the 1960s, maybe 1970s. Would you say that's a fair assessment?

I don't know. As I already said, the 1980s saw a pretty major development with the female detective. I'd throw *Murder, She Wrote* in there too, even though she's an amateur detective instead of a true private eye. And comic books have never let the detective go, like *Batman* or *Sin City*, and the 1990s was a banner time for comic books. So, I don't know that I'd cut it off completely in the 1970s, even if there's been some decline.

There's obviously still an audience for the private eye story in print, but it doesn't seem to hold the same kind of stature it once did. What changed in audience sensibilities? What changed in the market?

One thing might be the public's relationship to the police. In the early part of the 20th Century, there was a lot more anti-police sentiment across all parts of society. They were seen as tools of the system that was keeping everyone down, and their corruption was taken for granted, so outlaws and people working for a moral code instead of for the state were more acceptable heroes. Even many of the police stories in the pulps have as their protagonist a police officer who doesn't exactly follow orders, operating almost as a private detective within the system. And while corruption is still taken for granted and there are segments of society that still hate the police, such as in impoverished urban environments, overall, the role of the police as protectors and a positive force has come to dominate public opinion, especially post-9/11 when the police were truly heroes. People in real life are more inclined to go to the police with a problem than to a private detective now, so the kinds of cases real private detectives handle have become limited as well. As a result, police drama in literature, television, and film has come to represent much of the detective drama.

My editor, Charles Ardai, also points out that the advancement of forensic science has made it almost impossible for a lone private investigator to run a successful investigation. Crime detection relies heavily on fingerprinting, fiber analysis, DNA testing, and a private investigator just isn't going to have the resources needed to do that kind of forensic work. When Holmes was doing his own forensics, he was the only one doing it, so he could do it alone, but even in the BBC depiction of the character, he relies on the pathologist and other police resources.

When one thinks of the iconic literary private eyes – Hammett's Nick Charles and Sam Spade, Chandler's Philip Marlowe, Mickey Spillane's Mike Hammer, Ross Macdonald's Lew Archer – there doesn't appear to have been a P.I. character with that kind of dramatic weight since. Why do you think that is?

Again, I'd really throw Batman out there as the exception to that, even if his first appearance predates all of those characters. His current hold on the public is stronger than most of the other detectives have ever been. But Batman and the continuation of other characters developed in the earlier period withstanding, I, again, would argue that the type hasn't disappeared, just their profession. The same way the hardboiled figure appeared in Westerns before private eye books, and are now usually police officers or superheroes. And perhaps, as people began to have greater trust in the police, the idea of someone who works outside of the law has become more suspect (this contradicts my Batman point, of course). Instead of cheering on or wishing to be Mike Hammer, maybe now we see him as someone who's out of control, a bad element in society.

P.I. stories may be more of a niche genre these days, but they obviously still have their following. What is it about the private eye that still hooks a reader?

Mysteries in general are popular because they pose a question with very high stakes, and then give a satisfying answer. They horrify and reassure. So, regardless of who the detective is, whether private or public or military, people are attracted to mysteries. And so, most mystery lovers won't care whether the detective is private or public. So, it might be hard to say whether there are any specifics unique to the private eye that draws people in.

A lot of P.I. fiction being turned out today seems to echo the hardboiled, noirish style of an earlier literary age. Why do you think that is? Is it nostalgia for a certain kind of storytelling? Or is it that hard to find a contemporary voice that works for that kind of fiction?

Some of it is definitely nostalgia. Some of it is because people today are often more passive and equivocating than people were in the 1930s and 1940s. A male twenty-five year old in the 1940s didn't question whether he was a man or not, while many male twenty-five-year-olds today don't feel that they are men at all. So, it's much harder to believe that a self-assured man of action could do the things we expect fictional detectives do without a lot of formal training as a police officer, in the military, or in martial arts. That's why so many of the lone vengeance movies are (about) former military trainees.

By and large, people are reading less for entertainment, the big movers are titles of the fantastic and supernatural which appeal to younger readers. What's the future for the literary private eye?

First, from what I understand about the explosion of e-books, not to mention all of the reading that's done online, I'm not sure that people are actually reading less for entertainment. It's true that fantasy sells big, and, as a result, you'll find a lot detective stories written in fantasy worlds, like Jeff VanderMeer's work, so perhaps the future is that kind of genre bending. But just like *Deadwood* brought back the Western in Hollywood, I'm sure there will be a detective story that brings private eyes back as well.

CRIME FICTION:
A GOLDEN EAR
George V. Higgins and
The Friends of Eddie Coyle

One of the signatures of the "hardboiled" school of crime fiction is the volleys of sharp, clipped dialogue between characters. Think Dashiell Hammett, James M. Cain, Raymond Chandler, and their more modern-day descendants such as Evan Hunter (writing as Ed McBain) and Ross Macdonald. At their best, their terse, punchy dialogue flies back and forth like a match between tennis aces. But then in 1970, along came one-time assistant district attorney turned crime fiction author George V. Higgins who turned the hardboiled template on its ear with his debut novel, *The Friends of Eddie Coyle*.

All the usual tools of prose storytelling – exposition, interior thought, physical description – are minimalized by Higgins, when not done away with completely for great stretches. Instead, all those functions are carried out by dialogue. It's as if the Hemingway of "Hills Like White Elephants" were writing crime fiction…but then not quite. Higgins' characters talk…and talk and talk and talk. If the characters in traditional crime stories (or Hemingway, for that matter) trade shots, Higgins' characters trade extended barrages. The heroes of Hammett and Chandler et. al. dish out one-liners, while Higgins' protagonists exchange monologues. Acclaimed crime fiction author Dennis Lehane, in his introduction to the 2010 edition of *Eddie Coyle*, estimates that as much as "…a good eighty percent of the (182 page) novel…" is dialogue.

Take Higgins' introduction of the titular character. Eddie Coyle is a bottom dweller in the Boston area crime world, a little guy trying to hustle his way out from under a pending bootlegging sentence by pinballing between a quietly threatening Treasury agent, a piss-and-vinegar gun runner, a two-faced mobbed-up saloon keeper, and a gang on a bank robbing spree Coyle is supplying with guns. Typical of Higgins, Coyle is not so much a main character as the hook on which the author hangs an artfully shambling plot, but even at that Coyle is introduced with no more description than "The stocky man." As often happens in Higgins, the most salient characteristic about Coyle comes out of Coyle's own mouth. Trying to knock some of the starch out of young gun runner Jackie Brown, Coyle tells him:

> "Count your fucking knuckles"...
> "All of them?" Jackie Brown said.
> "Ah Christ," the stocky man said. "Count as many of them as you want. I got four more. One on each finger. Know how I got those? I bought some stuff from a man that I had his name, and it got traced, and the man I bought it for, he went to M C I Walpole for fifteen to twenty-five. Still in there, but he had some friends. I got an extra set of knuckles. Shut my hand in a drawer. Then one of them stomped the drawer shut..."

Coyle then goes on for two extended paragraphs on the pains and penalties of even an unintended slip. "I'm running short of fingers,' he concludes, "And if I gotta leave town, my friend, you gotta leave town."

More than any exposition or descriptive prose, these kinds of self-revealing tales – and the novel is rife with them – are what give the reader a handle on Higgins' characters. Coyle's stories, for instance, have the weight of years, of a tough, short-money life lived at the lowest rungs of criminality under the constant threats of arrest, betrayal, and violence. The wear and tear is showing. "I'm getting old," he tells Jackie Brown. "I spent my whole life sitting around in one crummy joint after another with a bunch of punks like you, drinking coffee, eating hash, and watching other people take off for Florida while I got to sweat how the hell I'm going to pay the plumber next week." Higgins never physically describes Coyle, but page by page, we get the slump-shouldered, heavy-footed, grunts-when-he-gets-to-his-feet sense of the man through what he reveals about himself through such dialogue.

Conversations in *Eddie Coyle* are circuitous, digressive, evasive. Every time Dillon the mob barman meets with Treasury agent Foley, their conversations drift – literally – for pages before they even begin to hover around the reason for the meeting. Representative example: Dillon meets with Foley to talk about a possible connection between Coyle and the bank robbers, but the exchange wanders for three irrelevant pages through the merits of tea *v.* coffee, the sale of porn magazines, and a well-to-do acquaintance of Dillon's who treated him to a Super Bowl trip. Only then is the topic at hand finally – though tentatively — addressed.

Even when Higgins' characters get to the point, they never quite get to the point. It's as if not quite saying something explicitly leaves them a psychological loophole, particularly when – in this world where, supposedly, nothing is worse than being an informant for the authorities – it seems so many of the characters are constantly trying to negotiate a deal with the cops. These exchanges are verbal waltzes, with each character dancing around the other to the music of Higgins' flavorful dialogue.

Ultimately, what "sells" these verbal tides is their sense of authenticity. According to true crime author and screenwriter Nicholas Pileggi *(Wise Guy* aka *Goodfellas; Casino)*, he recalls that Higgins once stated he was using wiretap recordings of conversations between real-life hoods as the model for his dialogue. According to Pileggi: "I think (Higgins) was one of the first writers that got inside the dialogue of the station house or courtroom."

It is because Higgins relies so heavily on dialogue to execute story functions that the one time he does go into a psychological interior, the occasion becomes a glaring – and calculated – interruption in the established voice and vantage of the novel.

The first in a series of bank robberies is told from the viewpoint of Samuel Partridge, vice president of the target bank. Partridge comes down for breakfast to find his family being held hostage by the masked gang, and told that while one man stays with his family, the rest of the crew will accompany him to the bank. At the bank, Partridge stands with one of the armed men waiting for the vault's time lock to open, his eyes fixed on the pistol in the robber's hand. As he waits on the time lock, Partridge's mind wanders to an occasion that past summer when he had rented a lakeside cabin for his family.

Partridge recalls taking his son fishing, then on returning to the cabin, as he begins collecting his fishing gear from the boat: "On the loose gravel of the shore, perhaps a foot from the stringer of fish, a thick brown timber rattler was coiled." Higgins then spends a half page describing the snake; its "glossy and dark" eyes, its flicking black tongue, its creamy underside, all with the same fear-generated-adrenaline-fueled startling detail and clarity with which Partridge has fixed the pistol in the hand of the man standing beside him at the vault door.

Partridge's memory of the snake – how even though it eventually slithered off, the knowing it was in the area would haunt the rest of his family's stay at the cabin – constitutes a break of two full pages in the bank robbery chapter. Not only is it the only time Higgins goes into a character's interior, but it is also the only time he breaks up one of his chapter-long scenes in such a manner.

Partridge is one of the few "civilians" in the novel, neither cop nor con. For the others, violence is a way of life, routine, not even worth remarking on other than as how to avoid being on the receiving end. But Partridge has none of those reference points, and Higgins sends the banker's memory off to the only other remotely similar threat in his life. The digression obliquely but emphatically illustrates how alien Partridge is to the world of Eddie Coyle and his "friends." One could even take the point that the reason Higgins spends that kind of time "inside" Partridge is because Partridge may be the only character with any interior life at all.

Coyle, the robbers, even the cops tracking them are all moves, countermoves, deals and counteroffers. There are no summers at a cabin with their families, but a hideout in a seedy trailer park with an oversexed mistress, and a few small-dollar deals to kep a family off the dole.

As blabby and indirect as Higgins' storytelling is, his work is as hardboiled as any Chandler or McBain or any of the other members of the hardboiled school. The sociopathic conduct of his characters, steeped in the air of this-is-how-it-really-is, self-described in Higgins' dancing dialogue, combine to produce the hardest of hard edges on *The Friends of Eddie Coyle*.

ROMAN NOIR:
RAISING CAIN
Charles Ardai on James M. Cain's
The Cocktail Waitress

Hammett, Chandler, Cain: the modern mystery thriller starts with them. They are the godfathers of that sensibility that would come to be called noir which would, in time, overflow the printed page and onto the stage, the big screen, and eventually even to television. Identified primarily with mysteries, the concept of flawed human beings ethically tripping and stumbling in a moral No Man's Land, equidistant between Right and Wrong, Good and Bad would bleed across genre lines. There would be noir Westerns (*Blood on the Moon*, 1948), noir war movies (*Attack!*, 1956), noir horror (*The Body Snatcher*, 1945), even noir melodramas like Cain's own *Mildred Pierce*, adapted for the screen in 1945.

But they all started with what Hammett, Chandler, and Cain did on the page, and each provided an evolutionary step which took what had once been usually dismissed as a flyweight genre dedicated to colorful private investigators and clever puzzles, and turned it into literature's dark star: stories that were less about cleverness than they were about recognizable, identifiable, relatable corruption.

Hammett came first, writing five novels between 1929 and 1934, but it was his third – *The Maltese Falcon* – which arguably had the greatest impact on the thriller genre. *Falcon*'s hero, private eye Sam Spade, redefined the P.I. hero. This was no intellectual superman, like Doyle's Sherlock Holmes, no bit of Agatha Christie whimsy. Spade was working class, a plodding pay-by-the-day dick, a knight errant loyal to a battered code of honor who realized there wasn't always a happy ending, and that justice came with a price – even to the just.

But there was still a touch of the exotic to Spade, and, in fact, much of Hammett's mystery fiction i.e. *The Glass Key*, *The Thin Man*. Hard-boiled and working class as Spade was, he was still in a world of not exactly run-of-the-mill hoods chasing after a jewel-encrusted statue.

Raymond Chandler introduced us to P.I. Philip Marlowe in the 1939 novel, *The Big Sleep*, and took him through seven more novels including the unfinished Poodle Springs in 1959 (Robert B. Parker would complete the novel in 1989). Marlowe was a more evolved Sam Spade: more contemplative, more philosophical, and, for that reason, a bit more world-weary and his battered code of honor even more battered.

But James M. Cain did them both one better.

He published his first thriller – the classic *The Postman Always Rings Twice* – in 1934 and followed it with a hot streak that didn't peter out until 1951; a run which included his two other great works, *Double Indemnity* and *Mildred Pierce*.

There were no jeweled dinguses at stake in Cain's novels, no family curses, and his heroes were not hard-drinking, chain-smoking, P.I.s or dogged cops. Instead, Cain's protagonists were startlingly unremarkable: an insurance salesman and a stifled housewife in *Indemnity*, a drifter and the wife/waitress to a diner owner in *Postman*. They weren't looking for The Big Score, they weren't even particularly criminals. They were people who stood at the edge of the moral abyss and, in a moment of weakness, gave in to that dark impulse to jump in, and almost instantly regretted it.

Our pop culture friends over at Titan Books have uncovered James M. Cain's last, unpublished novel, *The Cocktail Waitress*, released this month. Joan Medford is a typical Cain protagonist: a widow at 21; the accidental death of her alcoholic, abusive husband not quite accidental enough for one overeager cop; left broke; her young son in the custody of her less-than-sympathetic sister-in-law. Without even enough money to keep her house lights on, the unskilled Medford turns to pushing booze as a (if you haven't guessed it) cocktail waitress.

And also, like any Cain protagonist, Joan Medford missteps. Judgment gets clouded by romance, by sex, by her desperation to do right by her son and win him back from her sister-in-law.

For fans of hard-boiled fiction, and particularly for James M. Cain aficionados, it's all here: the tough talk, earthy dames, shady fast-talkers, and a balancing act down the thin moral line with cold-hearted pragmatism on one side, outright greed and deception on the other, and temptation plucking at the wire.

But it should be said that for the non-die-hard fan, *The Cocktail Waitress* can be a disappointment. Though Cain was writing the novel in the mid-1970s and setting the story in 1960, the book feels woefully disconnected from its time. Women still talk about having a pregnancy "taken care of" but won't use the word abortion; people still get their news primarily from the radio. Even Cain's prose feels dusty and archaic. Strip out the few contemporary references, and *Waitress* could easily seem a work from the '40s.

Titan's boss fiction editor, Charles Ardai, generously shared some thoughts with us on James M. Cain, *The Cocktail Waitress,* and how Cain's influence continues to filter through popular entertainment...

Dashiell Hammett, Raymond Chandler, James M. Cain – these are considered the holy trinity of mystery writing, in particular that genre dubbed "hard-boiled fiction." What is it about The Big Three that makes them The Big Three, and what was distinctive about Cain's work?

Cain, Chandler and Hammett were the first crime writers to elevate hardboiled or noir fiction above the level of simple genre entertainment and make something truly wonderful out of it, something that commented on human struggle and desperation and despair every bit as eloquently as the finest literary novel, while never losing touch with the genre's two-fisted, crowd-pleasing roots.

Chandler and Hammett did it for the detective story, with their invention of Philip Marlowe and Sam Spade, respectively. Cain did it for the non-detective story, the story of people trapped in painful circumstances and committing crimes to get out of them, only to find themselves driven deeper than ever into suffering. All three men wrote novels that remain breathtaking reads more than half a century after being penned. Cain in particular harnessed the dark sexual energy of love affairs gone sour to produce some of the most chilling and visceral portraits ever committed to paper. So discovering a lost book by Cain – a new book, effectively – is truly an important find.

Cain is considered one of the founders of the roman noir, and that sensibility later spilled over into film: film noir. How did what Cain bring to the genre impact on other forms like film and, later, TV? Do you still see traces of it?

Cain's impact is still felt in any drama that tackles adultery and the dark ends it sometimes drives lovers to. Any time you see a movie or TV show in which a sweaty couple post-coitally discusses offing the lady's husband, taking the dead man's money, and running away together, that's Cain's voice you're hearing.

And more than that: Cain's there in the atmosphere of so many films where California itself is a character and femmes fatale languorously drape themselves over settees, cigarette smoke trailing up toward a lazily turning ceiling fan. Cain's there in the scene in the run-down diner by the side of the highway, where a waitress in a too-tight uniform trades wisecracks with truckers about burning the place down and running away with them, and she's not serious, except maybe she is.

Cain's gift to dialogue writers was the bank shot, the way two people can seem to be talking about something innocuous but really are talking about something else altogether, something that could get them arrested if they talked about it head-on. Cain's influence is very much still there, even when today's writers and directors don't realize who it is they're imitating.

Chandler and his private eye Philip Marlowe may have produced movies' most memorable noir icon – the world-weary gumshoe poking into the dark underside of his clients – but it seems to me that Cain was closer to what noir was really about: impressively average people who make one misstep, then dig themselves deeper into a hole in their effort to get out of it. The Cocktail Waitress seems very much in that vein. Is that what Cain was all about as a writer?

Cain was definitely more interested in the people who commit crimes and the consequences it has on their lives than he was in the men who track them down. Even in *Double Indemnity,* where the relentless insurance investigator has a principal role, the focus is on the poor sap who gets lured into committing murder by the woman he hungers for. The police and other investigators are obstacles to be overcome, dangers to be feared, embodiments of retribution; they loom in the shadows and finally come and get you (and, often, kill you). But the "you" here is always an ordinary man or woman facing an extraordinary situation, and doing so without the benefit of a gun or a badge. It's not the only noir story worth telling, but it's a hell of a good one, and Cain excelled at telling it.

The only other author who came close was the brilliant Cornell Woolrich (author of *Rear Window* and so many other noir classics). Between Cain and Woolrich, you have a catalogue of the way ordinary people's lives can be ruined, with an emphasis on The Man Who Should Have Known Better.

Considering the success – and classic status – of Cain adaptations like The Postman Always Rings Twice *(1946) and* Double Indemnity *(1944), it's surprising to me that more of his novels weren't turned into films. I think* Mildred Pierce *(1945) was the only other one of his twenty novels to be turned into a film. Any thoughts on why that might be?*

Well, the three books you named are his three best – it's not surprising that they've also made the most memorable films. But *The Butterfly* (1982) became a movie starring Stacy Keach and Pia Zadora, the posthumous novel *The Enchanted Isle* was filmed as *Girl In the Cadillac* (1995), the 1956 film *Slightly Scarlet* was inspired by *Love's Lovely Counterfeit*, and also in 1956 *Serenade* was filmed, with Mario Lanza as the opera-singer protagonist and Vincent Price in a supporting role. So there have been other Cain films – they just didn't become famous the way the big three did.

There were also some TV and radio adaptations, and foreign films. And, of course, plenty of noir-ish movies that are heavily indebted to

Cain, even if they don't credit him as the official source of the material.

For a guy writing hard-boiled fiction, Cain seemed – for his time – extraordinarily sympathetic towards women. Mildred Pierce and Joan Medford in The Cocktail Waitress *are women just trying to take care of their families, but forced to extremes by circumstance. Even the femmes fatale of* Double Indemnity *and* The Postman Always Rings Twice *have a sympathetic quality to them: women who made a bad decision and now feel trapped into going as far as murder to get out of it. You can't even call Cora in* Postman *particularly greedy – the prize for all the conniving and murder is a roadside café. How do Cain's women characters stack up against the noir standard?*

It's true that Cain's women are sympathetic in a way the femme fatale types in crime fiction so often are not. That's partly just the touch of a better writer, the sort who can put Shylock in a play but not without giving him the "Hath not a Jew eyes?" speech. Cain's women aren't two-dimensional because he wrote about three-dimensional characters, and that's a big part of the reason (his) books hold up so well after all this time.

But it's true that he seems to have a genuine touch of sympathy in his soul for the hardships of being a woman in the 1930s, '40s, '50s, when marriage could be the only path available, and yet could prove to be more a trap than an opportunity. His women were what they were because their circumstances left them with few or no other options, not because they were the female equivalent of mustache-twirling villains. These aren't comic-book Cruellas toying with men for the sheer pleasure of villainy, or for perverse sexual satisfaction. They're desperate people trapped in dire situations, grasping at a last chance for something better. Unfortunately, the "something better" comes at a terrible price, and turns out to be much, much worse.

In your Afterword to The Cocktail Waitress, *you note that Cain's career "…which had risen so meteorically in the 30s and 40s had fallen just as meteorically." What was it about his work that had clicked so well with the reading public early on, and then had stopped working by the early '50s?*

I think these things just come in cycles. How many authors who were meteorically popular in the 1980s are still a hot number today? If Bret Easton Ellis penned a book in the '80s or '90s, it made headlines; he's still around today, still writing, but the headlines have passed him by.

Cain similarly made a splash in his day, and the ripples kept spreading for a good ten or twenty years, which is nothing to sneeze at. But by the late '50s and '60s, Cain's splash had been a generation back, and the new generation had writers of their own to get excited over.

Then, too, Cain really only published one book in the 1950s, *Galatea*, and it was a weak one, a real misfire. His next book after that didn't come out for nine more years. A decade is a long time to go between books and still keep your name out there, especially in the days before the Internet and social media, when word-of-mouth traveled so much slower and less efficiently.

After publishing a dozen mostly excellent books in the '30s and '40s (and one in 1951, but let's count that as the '40s for our purposes), Cain began a dry spell that lasted the rest of his life: just one book in the '50s, just two in the '60s, just two in the '70s, and none of them at the level of his earlier work. It's no surprise than the public's excitement about him waned.

According to your notes in The Cocktail Waitress, *Cain wrote that novel in the mid-1970s. The novel seems strangely disconnected from its time. Do you think one of Cain's problems, in the latter part of his career, was that he'd fallen out of step with the times?*

All old men are out of step with their times. They grew up in an earlier era and still view the present through the lens they ground in the past. Cain may have been writing *The Cocktail Waitress* in the 1970s, but it's so very clearly not a book about a world that contains discos and Olivia Newton-John and Atari and *Star Wars*. Various events in the book date it back to the late '50s/early '60s – basically the *Mad Men* era – but in terms of atmosphere and flavor, it sometimes feels like it takes place in the high noir era — the James M. Cain era, if you will — of the 1930s or '40s. Sure, there are passing references to hot pants and joints where the waitresses serve drinks topless…but the world of the book is the world Cain knew, the world of his prime.

During a trip to London in the book, the characters are talking about the wreckage in London left over from the Blitz. This is not a 1970s book. But does that make him out of step with his time? Or does it just make him a period novelist? The book is stronger for not being peppered with 1970s-iana. Reading it today, it's not dated, it's timeless. If it had been more 'in step' with its time when he wrote it, it may well be unreadable today.

It's sometimes said Ross Macdonald took his cue from Chandler. In film and TV, as well as on the page, do you see anyone picking up Cain's torch?

Macdonald definitely did pick up Chandler's torch, and then Lawrence Block picked up Macdonald's – the Matthew Scudder detective novels are the best and most important since Marlowe and Lew Archer. Who's done that for Cain's situations and themes?

Well, in the '50s and '60s, it was writers like David Goodis and Jim Thompson and Charles Williams and Gil Brewer, though no one of them burned as brightly. And today?

The best noirist working the Cain beat today is probably a woman named Megan Abbott, who has won the Edgar Allan Poe Award, deservedly, and has earned raves for each of her six books. She started out writing period noir fiction clearly influenced by Cain, and since has moved on to modern-day novels where the Cain influence is subtler. But it's there, and no other writer working in the genre today quite captures the feverish intensity and the lineaments of desire quite the way Megan does. Her prose makes me breathe faster, the way Cain's does.

That's on the page. On screen? Obviously, what Matthew Weiner has done on *Mad Men* is extraordinary. At the movies, you see noir less often than you used to – I guess spandex-clad superheroes and animated, quipping animals rake in the bucks better than homicidal lovers. But every so often you get a good one. I still tell my friends to track down John Dahl's *The Last Seduction* (1994), starring Linda Fiorentino. I think Cain would have been proud to call that one his own.

WAR STORY:
BEEN THERE, DONE THAT
Richard Herman and *The Peacemakers*

It's a familiar formula: a small group of underequipped soldiers at some isolated, Godforsaken outpost, surrounded and outnumbered by a savage enemy, hobbled by masters isolated by thousands of miles and self-interest from the bloody consequences of their politicking and diplomatic maneuvering. And then comes a third act catharsis as our little band of heroes-by-circumstance go rogue in an all-or-nothing fight for some greater, altruistic good.

As predictable a template as this may be, it's malleable enough to be stretched by exceptionally deft hands. On film, the range runs from a battlefield classic like *Zulu* (1964), to the comic book sensibility of *Rambo: First Blood II* (1985). On the page, there is Richard McKenna's powerful 1962 epic novel, *The Sand Pebbles*, on one end of the scale; with the simplistic, heavy-handed, flag-waving political thrillers of Tom Clancy on the other. Somewhere between McKenna and Clancy sits Richard Herman and *The Peacemakers*.

Since 1990, Herman, a retired Air Force officer with 21 years of service under his belt, has turned out a string of action-adventures, most of which, like Clancy's novels, wed the thrills to topical subjects. In the case of *The Peacemakers*, Herman focuses on a small Air Force unit of cargo planes providing supplies to refugees in war-torn southern Sudan. Lieutenant Colonel David Allston is their maverick commander who, faced with the corruption of his U.N. overseers and appalled by the savagery of Janjaweed raiders and their Sudanese Army sponsors, exceeds his mandate for neutrality, and, with a sympathetic unit of French Foreign Legionnaires, takes up the refugees' fight.

In terms of craft, Herman demonstrates two particular strengths worth noting: the kind of detail which the usual research strategies cannot provide, but which give the storytelling a vibrant realism; and a near-elegant construction for his extended action sequences, particularly the climactic engagement which spans 40 pages of the novel's 293 pages.

As for the former, the broad strokes of the situation in southern Sudan as well as the military hardware utilized in the story are available to any diligent online researcher, but Herman goes a step further. According to the author:

> *I also like to talk to folks who were actually there and cue off their experiences…I interviewed three C-130 crew members who flew relief missions in the Sudan…They told me about the widespread corruption in the UN relief effort…Further, they had many photos of the places depicted in the story, which helped to create a sense of place.*

And, of course, Herman has his own experience as a military officer, a flyer, an African Area Specialist for the Air Force, a veteran of two tours in Vietnam, and particularly that of someone who flew numerous relief missions in Africa in the 1960s, first in what was then The Congo, and later in Nigeria.

One manifestation of that first-hand on-the-ground experience is a thread of sub-Saharan discomfort running through the novel. Air conditioners labor, airfields are hot and dusty. When Allston first arrives at his command, the troops are ill-kempt as there isn't enough spare water for showers. A comfortable day is any day where the heat is less than brutal:

> "It's unusually cool this morning," Allston said…
> "Right," Lane agreed. "It must be all of eighty. Downright tolerable. Won't even break a sweat today." The two men laughed.

That discomfort is grimly amplified when Allston is first exposed to the plight of the refugees during his first relief flight:

> Dirty, gaunt-eyed children with swollen bellies sat in the dirt as flies swirled through the still, stifling, acrid air. Their eyes followed the Americans in silence…

Herman is even more familiar with the jockeying for position in the corridors of power. During a Pentagon briefing, a particularly political general – Yvonne Richards – watches a colonel on her staff misstep while briefing their superior, General Fitzgerald.

> (The colonel) had just told Fitzgerald what he already knew, not the best of beginnings, and missed the narrowing of Fitzgerald's eyes. But not Richards. The general's body language told her that he was not hearing what he wanted. Colonel Banks...was in danger of suffering a professional death by Power Point.

A paragraph later, Herman diagnoses the heart of the tedious colonel's problem as Fitzgerald muses, "A colonel's job was to think, evaluate, and react accordingly. This one was wasting his time."

That definition of a colonel's job; it is the regular flow of these small, insider's incidental details which give the novel a distinctive flavor setting it apart from others in the genre. Another example: Allston's investment in Australian bush hats to give his unit a jaunty sense of group identity. In an email, Herman told me, "…yes, the bit about the hats was corny, but believe me, it works."

And yet another example: Allston is faced with a female officer who is pregnant but refuses to leave her unit: "Allston did the one thing he had never done, and had hoped that he would never have to. He gave a direct order." For people outside the military, that giving a direct order would be such a rarity – as well as Allston's discomfort in having to give one – must be a striking revelation. Again, from Herman:

> *I served under many decent, competent commanders who most would consider good leaders. But a true leader is a very rare bird, and (the character of) Allston is one. They operate at a cut above the others...Allston did not have to give direct orders because he didn't need to. The troops understood the mission and willingly followed Allston into hell to accomplish it. In my book, that is true leadership.*

And then, of course, there's Herman's extensive flying experience. One can research what knobs to turn, what levers to push and pull, what gauges to read, etc., but those little details that come naturally to the experienced flyer are not always on the page or the Internet: "The copilot rechecked the landing gear and placed his left hand over (the pilot's) right hand on the throttle quadrant." Several years ago, advising me on a piece of my own writing, Herman had explained to me that the co-pilot's hand sits on the pilot's to keep the pilot's hand in place on the throttles should something happen which could possibly jar the pilot's hand from the controls.

A more conspicuous display of skill is Herman's handling of his action sequences, and the novel's Third Act offers his best demonstration. The final, all-out onslaught by Sudanese troops and Janjaweed on the refugee camp spans three chapters and 40 pages. The action revolves around several focal points: Allston, the Legionnaire commander Colonel Pierre Vermullen, and an occasional digression to Allston's security chief Malone, and Major Jill Sharp, one of Allston's staff.

The perennial problem for any writer depicting action is that we see faster than we read; it takes much longer to describe a piece of action than the few seconds – or even fraction of a second – it takes to see it. The challenge can be complicated by working with an action which may, in turn, be composed of a chaotic mix of multiple smaller acts. The goal for the author is to organize the chaos while still capturing at least some of the frantic quality of a desperate moment.

Herman manages this through a combination of several strategies. "I'm ex-Air Force and that means I'm anal," he told me, explaining that this results in a detailed outlining of a novel before he sets himself to write. As for the extended action finale:

> I have a mental picture of what is going on, and…figure out a
> way to describe it. The secret to getting an action sequence right
> is revision, revision, revision…I estimate I revised the finale of
> The Peacemakers at least thirty times.

This extensive revision practice produces action sequences which are both clear and precise.

> By the time I get to the final scene, not only have I outlined the
> action, I have brainstormed it, sat on a rock and cogitated, jotted
> down bits of dialogue, and flown the mission in my head.

Despite some frantic intercutting between the various focal points (these are more than simple transitions within the text; Herman makes clear breaks when switching from one locale to another), the separate threads read smoothly because Herman initially develops them independently and fully: "I wrote the Allston thread first, then came back and wrote the Vermullen thread."

And then, to capture the chaotic quality of the fight as well as accelerate the pace at key moments, Herman keeps each sequence "short and sharp."

At the beginning of the Third Act, as Allston's outfit prepares for the attack they know is coming, the opening pages of Chapter 24 are broken up into sequences averaging about a page and a half in length. About six pages into the chapter, as the action begins to heat up, the sequences begin to shorten, typically running about a page or so. Fourteen pages in, with Allston's people now fully engaged with an enemy pressing home the attack, cutting between locales comes faster, with sequences sometimes only a few paragraphs long, and even shorter.

One example: Allston is flying a makeshift gunship against enemy tanks that Vermullen is facing on the ground. Herman hangs on Allston for a single paragraph of 11 lines before switching to Vermullen's vantage for an even shorter paragraph of just three sentences.

Conversely, when the action hits a lull, Herman loosens the reins and the separate sequences again become longer and more full-bodied. Like an orchestra conductor speeding up and then slowing the tempo for effect, throughout those 40 pages Herman's sequences expand and segue smoothly from one to the other, then contract and move in abrupt jumps. It's a system that works not unlike editing patterns in action films, and, like that kind of editing, produces the same kind of visceral agitation which plays into the excitement and violence of the content.

The value of an insider's feel, and a structure carefully calibrated to bring up the pulse rate: these are two valuable lessons for the action writer offered up by Richard Herman's *The Peacemakers*.

MEMOIR:
BEING HIS OWN PUNCHLINE
Bill Persky and
My Life Is a Situation Comedy

I once wrote a series of novels narrated by a character who was a British journalist in WW II. The first novel in the series went through several drafts until I could hit on the right voice for the narrator. But, in creative nonfiction, one would think there should be no such hunt. In nonfiction, first person pieces are assumed to be in the voice of the person telling the story. I'm learning that's not always quite true, not in the strictest sense anyway.

David Sedaris, for example sets his "I" in an often odd, bizarre, and at times even grotesque universe, then inflates the weirdness with a controversial degree of fabulism. In interviews I've read with Sedaris, I've come to suspect his on-the-page "I" is something of a, well, not quite a put-on, but a construct, a character that may key off of Sedaris' sensibility, but is – like his stories – a manipulated bit of exaggeration. Then there's Tucker Max, his "I" probably best self-described by the title of one of his books: *Assholes Finish First*. There's an intentionally abrasive I'm-a-dick-and-damned-proud-of-it quality throughout his work, a more-or-less genre *The New York Times*' Warren St. John christened "fratire." There's a sense of artifice to Max's voice as well. He revels too much in the role of provocateur, seems overly intent on pushing PC buttons. It's hard to argue with the success of either writer, but it seems to put their work in the vein of "creative not-quite-fiction-not-quite-nonfiction."

I'm already inhibited in my attempts at first person nonfiction. I have an instinctive reluctance to reveal too much of myself, and techniques like those of Sedaris and Max strike me as exercises in camouflage rather than true first person engagement. From them I can only learn how to hide. I found the reverse to be true in *My Life Is a Situation Comedy*, a collection of 60 memoirish vignettes by Emmy-winning TV writer, producer, director Bill Persky. I have the benefit of having known the man for close to 30 years, so I can say that the man on the page is the man I know. From the pieces in *My Life...*, I've seen the value of an open, honest, self-effacing storytelling. Sedaris and Max may, arguably, be stronger prose artists, but there's a connection Persky makes with an almost ruthless vulnerability that they don't.

Persky has the benefit of being an inherently funny man. Here's him leading up to discussing his disastrous first marriage:

> I offer this scenario not with pride but in the interest of full disclosure as to how good I was with women going back to my first kiss with Esther Kastoriniss during a game of "mailman" at her eighth birthday party and then worrying that she had become pregnant...I doubt I was much better informed, or prepared, 20 years later when I embarked on my first marriage.

I remember Persky on a panel at NYU with the late Sid Caesar some years ago talking about writing for *The Dick Van Dyke Show*. Persky told the audience that the key to writing for the series was that almost every episode usually started with one of the writers coming into the office saying, "Let me tell you about what happened to me this weekend..." That life-sizedness was the hallmark of Persky's best work (which includes *That Girl* and *Kate & Allie)*. Similarly, in these prose pieces, rather than adapt some kind of persona, he consistently remains, despite his considerable success, determinedly average, addled by many of the same foibles most of us can identify with, and more than willing to expose them. Says Persky:

> *I am always cautious about revealing anything that might hurt others (but) I am fair game and outside of things that would hurt a future presidential run, I feel free to reveal all.*

While Persky's voice remains consistent throughout the stories, his tone does shift. His storytelling can be flat-out funny, but can also be incredibly poignant, as in telling about the time he was going to take his three-year-old daughter Dana to a charity event, with her excited about being escorted by noted "little person" actor Billy Barty. Just before the party, Dana's hand is accidentally crushed in a door. Persky rushes her to the hospital. Held up at a stoplight, he decides to check on her hand which he'd wrapped in a now blood-soaked towel:

> ...somehow I had to see. With teeth clenched and breath held I reached for the towel and as I gently started to unwrap it, (Dana) stopped crying, looked up and said, "Don't look at it, Daddy...it will hurt your eyes."

By shifting his tone just a few degrees, the same Persky tells a self-mocking story about trying to resuscitate his second marriage after he and his then wife had separated with her moving into their beach house:

> The call finally came, but it was an invitation for me to come to the beach on Saturday so we could "share our feelings"...it was the mid-70s and "share" had replaced the more mundane "talk about." I took a shot and told her I "knew where she was coming from," and Saturday was "cool." I had no shame.
> She said, "Right on."
> I threw in an "I can dig it," which I think was left over from the 50s, and hung up. It was Thursday so with just two days to get in shape, I immediately did four pushups followed by a Scotch and a cigarette.

Persky explained to me where those shifts in tone come from:

> *I live on two levels: one where I am doing what I am doing, and the other watching myself doing what I am doing. It is the observing me that is my voice. That "me" is constantly amazed, embarrassed, and amused at my behavior, but when I come across, usually unaware, of something bigger at stake, I tend to let the emotion or the gravity of the situation sit there on its own. Then, I probably observe myself doing that and get on with being entertaining and light to let it all stand on its own.*

Rather than put a wall up between himself and the reader through an alienating "otherness" (Sedaris), or by taking on the attitude of a commanding, justifiably (in his own mind) bragging *ubermensch* (Max), Persky lays himself bare. In one of the collection's strongest pieces which falls somewhere in the middle of his tonal range, he deftly mixes his wit with some witty ruminations on discovering "…the *real* you, the one you doubt, question, and hide from the world and with less success, from yourself." The occasion: sometime after five in the morning, a nude Persky is awakened by a burglar climbing through his bedroom window.

> I leapt naked from my bed, grabbed the first weapon at hand – my Ralph Lauren pillow – and went on the attack screaming "Get out! Get out!" in a high-pitched voice. I resented my mother speaking for me at a time like that and consciously tried to get into a lower register, one that had more indignation than fear, but it was her moment and I couldn't take it away from her.

Persky manages to fight the burglar off, and has a revelation:

> It isn't a question of courage, but of clarity, and the freedom that comes when you know you're right. In our daily lives, it's never as obvious as someone coming through our bedroom window. It's vague or obtuse, and our first instinct waits as we filter through too much information and conditioning, and we lose that first impulse, which is pure us.

I asked Persky if he exaggerated in any of the pieces for comic effect:

> *I think the "exaggeration" is part of the self-observation; I am enhancing my own absurdity…I am observing myself and then saying to myself, "You are pathetic" just a touch before the audience does…The most extreme example of this was when I was curled up in a sniveling ball at the foot of the bed, begging Betty, my second wife, not to leave me. Then, my observer self looked at me, evaluated the situation, and said to her, "Am I too macho?" We laughed, hugged, both cried, and she left in the morning. I love the part of me that can do that (although) I wouldn't mind losing the sniveling part.*

Any author worth his/her salt regularly strip-mines his/her experience for material, whether it's to find reality in a bit of fiction, or the drama (or comedy, or mix of both) in real life. For some writers, the line between both (Sedaris, Max) is fudged, and, depending on what the moral stakes are for a piece of material, perhaps that's of no particular concern. But for someone with the psychological blocks I have against self-revelation, Bill Persky's willingness to dissect himself (often leavened with a deft, comic touch) for our enjoyment offers a tutorial in the value of brutal honesty.

MEMOIR/CRITICAL ANALYSIS:

A LIFE REFLECTED IN ART; THE ART REFLECTED IN A LIFE

Kier-la Janisse and
House of Psychotic Women

One of a writer's most lethal enemies is familiarity; that early on, a reader already has a sense of the whole piece, killing the tension that creates suspense, mystery, anticipation. Kier-la Janisse's answer to the problem in her non-fiction work, *House of Psychotic Women: An Autobiographical Topography of Female Neurosis in Horror and Exploitation Films* (FAB, 2012), is to mash up two seemingly unrelated genres – an autobiography and a critical analysis of certain brands of low-end horror films – into one, provocative, surprisingly complete whole. The thematic glue holding these components together is the concept that our sensibilities – what we like and don't like, the value we see or don't see in creative work – are, at least to a large extent, shaped by the people who we are, and how we got to be that way.

Janisse, a writer and film programmer as well as the author of *A Violent Professional: The Films of Luciano Rossi* (FAB, 2007), is an anomaly: a fan of the kind of blood-drenched, low-budget movies which more typically appeal to young males, and persistently raise the ire of feminists with their depictions of women as victims (often in grotesque fashion), manipulating victimizers (ditto), and brutal avenging angels (ditto again). To throw a little more gas on the fire, Janisse is particularly fond of the made-on-the-cheap grindhouse fodder of the 1970s-early 1980s i.e. *Ms. 45* (1981), *Roadside Torture Chamber* (1972), and *Prey* (1977), as well as imports like *The Bird with the Crystal Plumage* (1970), and *The Blood-Spattered Bride* (1972).

But in these movies typically dismissed by much of high-brow, "serious" film criticism, Janisse finds chords resonant with her own scarred psyche. Born in 1972 in Winnipeg, "...an isolated city in the dead centre of Canada known for its long, harsh winters and its citizens' tragic propensity of alcoholism and violent crime," she suffered through, consecutively, abandonment by her birth parents, a philandering adoptive father, and a paradoxically emotionally abusive/supportive stepfather. Janisse has memories of a time between her mother's marriages of listening through her bedroom door to her mother being assaulted by an intruder. There's a parade of foster homes, self-destructive acting out, relationships in which she is sometimes the abused, other times the abuser, and an increasingly neurotic and eventually distant mother. She found her own real-life horrors reflected in distorted funhouse mirror fashion in the fetishistic gore of Italian *giallo*, drive-in exploitation flicks like *Ms. 45*, as well as in more nuanced, upscale work like *Whatever Happened to Baby Jane?* (1962) and *Persona* (1966). In these movies, Janisse "...found myself unconsciously drawn to female characters who exhibited signs of behavior I had recognized in myself: repression, delusion, jealousy, paranoia, hysteria."

Janisse writes with insight, power, passion, and style, whether she is discussing film – "Guilt ran through the 1970s genre films like a parasite, eating away at the psyches of female characters, who oscillated between domestic responsibility and the desire for autonomy" – or one of the many troubling yet colorful episodes from her life:

> ...given my erratic emotional and social patterns, my Christian Aunt Pam started to worry about my mental and spiritual well-being. After all, I was a sketchy juvenile delinquent with a gun living in the basement listening to *Anarchy in the UK* about a hundred times a day. One night...she and her weird friend Beth came down to my room...they were going to save my soul with the help of Jesus Christ. I was really tired and asked if they could save my soul some other time.

While, for the most part, the two threads of the book – autobiography and critical analysis — move in reflecting parallel, the connection between them does, at times, become manifest such as her discussion of the Italian 1974 creeper, *The Perfume of the Lady in Black:*

> There are a lot of elements from my own life playing
> themselves out in this film. Silvia's crazy work ethic, her
> independence, her collection of toys and other signifiers of
> stunted emotional development, her idolization of an absent
> father, her abuse at the hands of a substitute father-figure,
> and her consequent demonization of her mother for allowing
> it all to happen.

Manifest or not, that is the engine of the book: that Janisse views these horror shows – titles often dismissed as exploitive schlock by the cinematic mainstream – through the lens of her own personal horror show, and so, where others see exploitation, she finds a macabre brand of art.

House of Psychotic Women *combines two easily identifiable genres: an autobiography, and a genre analysis. Either one of those elements as you wrote them is strong enough to stand on its own. What was your thinking on putting the two together?*

I originally planned the book as a book of essays on specific films, which – at the time of the book's conception – were rare films. But, as I kept procrastinating about working on the book, the internet exploded and the cult DVD boom happened, and the films were suddenly being written about everywhere, very intelligently. So, I almost threw out the book, thinking there was no point in even writing it since there was already so much solid writing online on film sites and blogs.

But the duality of the book started to appear maybe in 2003. I started to revisit it, and even asked my dad (a psychologist) to write it with me. He was suspicious of the idea, so I dropped that pretty quick. But I thought perhaps I would have a sidebar running along every page that would have personal anecdotes in it, since I realized that a lot of the films had parallels in my own life story. But even then, they would not be integrated into the main text; instead, it would be more like a magazine that has sidebars or trivia or something running alongside the main article.

I think I dropped the book again for a few years, and then it was probably my friends Matthew Rankin and Caelum Vatnsdal who convinced me to pick it up again, and focus on the more personal elements. But I didn't know how to integrate these things.

I was influenced to a certain extent by James Ellroy's *My Dark Places,* and even Stanley Booth's *True Adventures of the Rolling Stones* in that they were each inserted into the story they were telling, while maintaining a lot of history, facts, and critical observations. But I would say when my friend Chandra Mayor gave me a copy of Sandy Balfour's *Pretty Girl in Crimson Rose* that the structure of *HOPW* really came into place.

Balfour's book is about cryptic crosswords, so I wasn't sure why Chandra had given it to me, but when I started reading it, I realized the structure was pretty much exactly what would make my book work. I mean, sometimes his transitions between crossword history and his memoir are overtly clunky – he'll be talking about a crossword and then say, "And that reminds me of a story!" and vice versa – and I didn't want my transitions to be as obvious as that, so I tried to integrate the two types of storytelling more, and even leave some things implied so that the reader could make the connections between things themselves. So, in a sense, I guess my structure is slightly more experimental, but it would never have existed without Balfour's book.

On the switching back and forth between the two threads: was there a plan? Or did it happen organically in the writing?

Some of it was planned, but a lot of the patterns and connections became apparent as I was writing. I would have these "Eureka!" moments where I realized certain things connected, and then I would shuffle things around.

It's quite a no-holds-barred memoir wedded to a genre often labeled as lurid and exploitive. Was there ever a concern that the one might color a reader's judgment of the other?

My two concerns about the structure were that it would seem really self-indulgent and narcissistic and that would turn readers off, but also,

I totally expected the horror community to turn on me. I was ready for all the bloggers to slag the book, to make fun of me, and when this didn't happen, I was shocked. I mean, the internet is a cruel place and here I was writing this totally personal book to be read by people who can be quite obsessive and critical. I truly expected everyone to hate it. But not only did the opposite happen – most of the notices have been positive – but it reached beyond the horror community, and all kinds of people buy it, whether they are film fans or not.

I've had people buy it off me at events for relatives who are mentally ill, or they are mental health professionals. I've had people buy it because they relate to the foster home stories. And strangely enough, some famous people have read it and posted about it online, which is totally bizarre and flattering to me.

The autobiographical sections are gutsy, to say the least. Did you ever have second thoughts about how open to be about yourself? Or did you consider that openness vital to the entirety of the book?

I knew I had to be candid or it wouldn't work. I'm talking about some serious psychological problems with many of the characters in the movies I discuss, so it wasn't enough to just say I could relate to them. I had to talk about why. I had to try to instill in the reader an understanding of these characters beyond the usual dismissal of craziness. I have empathy for these characters, and I wanted the readers to feel that.

That said, I haven't laid my entire soul bare; I still have some secrets. But none of the stories I kept to myself were really relevant to exploring the characters in the book. But, yeah, there's some pretty embarrassing stuff in the book. Some of my acquaintances had a hard time looking at me after they read it!

How therapeutic was it to deal with the events you discuss on the page in this way?

Lots of people ask me this. It was therapeutic for sure. I came out of it with way more empathy for my parents, and after a brief blow-up upon the book's release, it actually brought me closer to certain family members. But it also didn't provide "closure" in any traditional sense. There are still a lot of unanswered questions between me and my mom, things that will never be answered.

And I didn't come out of it "cured" from my neuroses (as an aside, I also love that most mental health professionals cringe at the outdated language I use in the book – apparently it's not called "neurosis" anymore). I still have a lot of problems staying calm, and being able to keep up a front of normality. It's exhausting. I can only act normal for a few hours and then I have to be alone where I don't have to monitor my obsessive mannerisms.

But, overall, I would say yes, it was cathartic, which is why I put the book out there even though I expected people to hate it.

TRUE CRIME:
AN INSIDE JOB
Sonny Grosso, Philip Rosenberg
and *Point Blank*

One of the most memorable set pieces in the Academy Award-winning 1971 cop thriller *The French Connection* (right behind the classic car chase sequence) features the film's stars, Gene Hackman and Roy Scheider, as two NYPD Narco detectives rousting a seedy ghetto neighborhood bar populated with nickel-and-dime dope peddlers and users in a manner that would set any ACLU lawyer's teeth on edge. If you were in the business of writing cop thrillers, it's not a procedure you'd find researching on the web or in true accounts of cops and copdom. You wouldn't even find it in author Robin Moore's account of the "French Connection" case which served as the basis for the movie. But it's true, it's real, and it was the kind of detail that made *Connection* the movie that changed cop movies forever.

I know this because Sonny Grosso, one of the real-life French Connection detectives (Scheider's character is based on Grosso; Hackman's on Grosso's partner, Eddie Egan), told me so. I interviewed him several years ago about the movie. He and Egan had spent several weeks with Hackman and Scheider showing them how street cops did things. The bar roust? Egan and Grosso had had the actors watch them do it for real from outside bars, then watch from inside the bars, then actually had them make the arrests. "Eddie must've done the thing in the bar a dozen times in those three weeks (we were with the actors)," Grosso told me. "I'd seen him do it a *thousand* times before."

The point being that research is well and good, and there are topics and eras too distant and/or long gone for whom the web and the library are our only tools. But other times...

I had the chance to interview Grosso again, this time about the differences between private eyes in movies and on TV and their real-life counterparts: "...(private investigators) I knew who hadn't been cops often teamed up with an ex-cop. There's just no way to learn that stuff on your own." According to Grosso, nothing prepared someone for work as a private investigator better than time on the force. That is advice the presumptive author of tales of cops and hoods should heed, because even the most diligent research can't quite bring the *feel* of being a cop – the mindset, the worldview – to a story like a real cop can. One of Grosso's favorite brags is telling about the reviewer who said *The French Connection* "...*smelled* like a real cop story."

I've seen what that kind of authenticity can do for a novel in a number of my previous close readings: one time criminal attorney George V. Higgins and his *The Friends of Eddie Coyle*, ex-spy John LeCarre and *The Russia House*, retired Air Force pilot Richard Herman and *The Peacemakers*. And for someone trying to hammer out his own story of cops and hoods, it came to me in this true account penned by Grosso and Philip Rosenberg. For this paper, I asked Grosso bluntly, "What can an author learn working with a cop that he/she can't get from research?"

"Six million fucking things."

Joe Longo was a veteran detective with one of the NYPD's Narcotics units who became entangled in one of a number of anti-corruption schemes which sprang up in the wake of the Knapp Commission revelations about police corruption in the early 1970s. Longo was clean, but the distorted nature of the snare as well as the almost sociopathic overzealousness of the government officials behind it made Longo's guilt or innocence irrelevant. The sting left Longo vulnerable to what amounts to extortion by higher-ups to become an informant in further anti-corruption snares.

For most of us, our perception of cops and how they do their jobs (or fail to) has been shaped by a near-incessant barrage of popular images in movies and on TV over the years, from the seedy, corrupt cop, to the door-kicking Dirty Harry-esque vigilante cop, to the committed Good Cop who eventually gets his man while bumping up against (while begrudgingly obeying) what often seem unfair, hood-friendly rules. Any season of any of the *Law & Order* brands is guaranteed to give you that whole cop buffet.

But *Point Blank* presents a more morally ambiguous universe, one in which even the most well-intentioned cop (whether he's fighting narcotics or police corruption) operates in a moral twilight zone. The delineations between right/wrong, good/bad are fudged and shaded. Take Grosso/Rosenberg's analysis of the issue of illegal wiretapping:

> ... in most cases illegal wiretapping is the product of laziness or impatience rather than corrupt motives. A detective who is willing to take the time and trouble can get a court order for a wiretap whenever he needs one. The paperwork alone may involve half a day's work, and another day can be spent waiting to see a judge. But in the end the cop will get his wiretap order. Of course, many cops, unwilling to waste this much time, elect to short-circuit the system, using legal wires only when they want to be able to bring the tapes into court as evidence. In the early stages of an investigation, when they are interested merely in finding out what a suspect is up to, they cheat on the law.

At another point in the book, the authors go so far as to say, "... the major reason for the prevalence of illegal wiretapping is the fact that superior officers tacitly – and in some cases openly – encourage their investigators to use all means possible to get results." Not exactly the picture of hand-wringing and finger-wagging over toeing the Constitutional line one sees on prime time TV.

One of the book's more enlightening passages deals with that phenomenon so often depicted in stories about dirty cops; the unwillingness of their fellow cops to point a finger. It's such a trope of the dirty cop scenario, we often take it as a given without quite understanding (or maybe even becoming frustrated by) why someone charged with law enforcement would allow another law officer to go on the take. Grosso (and this section seems more Grosso than Rosenberg) presents a cop's-eye view on this:

> You didn't judge him because you knew what the temptations

were. It was a world full of desperate men, addicts and pushers and stools, users who'd rat on their pushers for the price of a fix, dealers who kept themselves in business by selling out the guys they bought from, stools who'd hand up their connections to get you off their backs and then hand you up to the shooflies (Internal Affairs) for the same reason. If you didn't take it on the chin you'd get it up the ass, either way, banged and double-banged. In the last analysis that was why you had to be the exception, why all cops had to be. In the vast, pulsing spider web of betrayal, cops had to stand together, had to have each other to trust.

Grosso also told me a cop source can provide insight into the sometimes intricate machinations involved not only in police work, but in trying to get police *not* to do their work. *Point Blank* outlines one such stratagem as Gil Lacey, a cop working as an informant for anti-corruption hunters, unsuccessfully attempts to bribe Longo to compromise a case:

Lacey's proposal depended on a little-known technicality of police and courtroom procedure. An agent working on a case fills out daily report forms detailing his activities...Although they are not regarded as documentary evidence and are not subject to discovery motions by the defense, copies of them are given to defense counsel if the agent who originally filed them takes the stand during the trial.

Lacey intended to use the phony reports for a defense counsel but provide them too late for them to do his client any good, an arrangement Grosso/Rosenberg describe as "almost elegant."

Point Blank also captures the obsessive zeal of those running anti-corruption operations. These are hardly white knights looking to clean up the department. Rather, they're high-ranking cops, administrators, and attorneys who've developed their own skewed view of the universe. Finding out that Longo, a detective with an impeccable record, had worked Narcotics, was enough for one of the high-rankers behind the case to declare, "...as far as I'm concerned they're all a bunch of fucking thieves." Once Longo is drawn into the sting, the same official tells

Longo flatly, "…you only got three choices. You can work with us, you can go to jail, or you can blow your brains out. Take your pick."

According to Grosso, "It could be a tennis player or a bowler or a writer, it doesn't matter, but the real guys brings so many things that are interesting" to the table that even the most energetic research can't match the nuance, the authenticity, the *smell* of the real thing that can only come from someone who's been there and done it.

TRUE CRIME:
COP'S EYES
Adam Plantinga and
400 Things Cops Know

"Cop's eyes." Reading Adam Plantinga's *400 Things Cops Know: Street-Smart Lessons from a Veteran Patrolman* brought the phrase back to me. It was something out of a string of books about police I'd read years ago – the title escapes me – but I've never forgotten it: "Cop's eyes." The writer was referring to the way a cop's eyes never settle, even when they're in a casual conversation, even off duty. They're always looking, studying, wary. But Plantinga's book made me think about the concept in a larger, more expansive sense; not just as a form of observational restlessness, but as a worldview. Plantinga knows that worldview well: he spent seven years as a police officer in Milwaukee, and is currently serving as a sergeant with the San Francisco P.D.

Cops don't live in the same world you and I do. Theirs is a world of victims and victimizers, liars, thieves, deceivers, the casually brutal, more kinds of crazy than you can count. They work among the dead, the dying, the assaulted, and those who did the killing and the assaulting. "Sometimes," writes Plantinga, "you learn stuff you wish you didn't know. Sometimes you wish you could turn it all off." No wonder, then, that with that kind of psychological wear and tear, "...police officers are six times more likely to kill themselves than the general public, a figure that more than triples after retirement...The divorce rate for cops in big city departments is...by some estimates as high as 80 percent." It also explains why cops sometimes do things that bring out the protesters and even leave the non-protestors wondering, "What was going through that cop's head?"

I happened to pick up Plantinga's book at a singularly appropriate time. We're still dealing with the aftershocks of the Michael Brown shooting in Ferguson, Missouri, and the chokehold death of Eric Garner in New York, as well as the assassination of two New York City cops by an apparently deranged man claiming he killed to avenge the deaths of Brown and Garner. The six months encompassing those events have involved a lot of finger-pointing and yelling and screaming and blaming, cops being defensive, TV camera hogs calling for one kind of silver bullet or another to prevent the next Ferguson; better training, more strict policies on the use of force, racial balance in police forces, etc. What Plantinga's book makes clear – at least to me – is that the discussion that needs to happen isn't the current shouting match. The one that needs to happen probably is never going to happen.

It's a running theme in cop literature that cops live in an insular world, one in which the only people who understand cops are other cops, and they're not wrong, at least not completely. How can you understand the worldview of a man or woman who "...will see more human tragedy in the first three years of their (police) career than the average person will see in a lifetime"? Their missteps and excesses become front page news, fodder for second-guessing in every editorial column and Sunday morning TV gabfest. People outside the cop world want cops to do better; cops inside the cop world answer you're lucky it works as well as it does.

I saw those worldviews bump up against each other a couple of weeks ago when I caught a few minutes of an episode of *Dr. Phil* in which the subject was police conduct. In the interest of showing that incidents like the Brown shooting weren't always all about race, one of the guests was a white guy whose unarmed brother had been shot by a cop, also white. Phil's guest called for a policy where cops shouldn't use deadly force until a threat to their lives was clear. Which, on the surface, sounds reasonable. Except...

I hadn't read Plantinga's book yet, but I've known cops, I've been related to a couple, and I'd read enough cop lit to know what a cop's response would be: If I wait that long and there is a threat, after I've given the other guy that kind of head start, I'm not going home.

In other words, it's a more complicated issue than I think either side appreciates. And it may be a problem without a solution, because what's wanted – what's needed – might very well be impossible. "To really do this job right," says Plantinga, "you need the serene self-possession of a Tibetan monk...be crafty like LBJ. Fast like Jackie Joyner. Principled like Serpico. You must deliver unbearable news with the sensitivity of Clara Barton. You have to hit like Hagler. Of course, no one can be or do all of these things." Plantinga later concludes, "...you wonder if it's a job anyone is really suited to fill."

•

The canon of cop lit is broad and deep, ranging from novels like *The New Centurions* and *The Blue Knight* from Los Angeles cop Joseph Wambaugh, to non-fiction works like David Simon's *Homicide: A Year on the Killing Streets*. My book shelf includes Harvey Rachlin's *The Making of a Cop* which follows three NYPD wannabes through their application, screening, training, and probationary period; Connie Fletcher's *What Cops Know*, a collection of cop wisdom based on interviews with members of the Chicago P.D.; and, in my view, one of the best of the lot, Mark Baker's *Cops: Their Lives in Their Own Words*, a collection of interviews with cops from departments large and small across the country, broken up into categories from the routine to matters of life and death.

But Adam Plantinga's book stands alone. The structure of the book is right there in its plain-spoken title: *400 Things Cops Know*. Elegantly simple, the book is an it-only-looks-simple series of category lists ('18 Things Cops Knows about the Use of Force," "28 Things Cops Know About Booze and Drugs," "21 Things Cops Know About Thugs and Liars," etc.). Plantinga delivers these things cops know in write-ups ranging from fortune cookie brevity ("Fights between teenage girls often start with one girl saying, "Heard you've been talking about me"), to pieces long enough to qualify as essays.

I say it only looks simple because what emerges from these little, superficially disconnected pieces is a larger, nuanced, complex portrait of the life cops lead: one in which the young, idealistic cop must fight against the corrosive effect of constantly dealing with people at their worst...or most insane. And then, as one little capsule of cop wisdom piles on another, one also begins to divine Plantinga's own story; his own, youthful, idealistic days, his own individual experiences, his own creeping cynicism and fatalism, his own struggle to hold on to compassion. Any reader of cop lit will be familiar not only with the arc but with a lot of what Plantinga has to say, but his approach – building up that cop world brick by brick around the reader – ultimately feels more immersive and vital than most conventional narratives.

Of course what makes the concoction work and keeps it from being nothing more than a dry rendering of things-cool-to-know is Plantinga's droll, underplayed but never dry prose. Patrol is about the crazy, the horrifying, and the heart-breaking being all part of another day on the street, and the only way to psychologically survive is to keep emotions on a short leash, not dwell, and move on to the next assignment. Very often, the poignancy that is also a part of *400 Things* is in that restraint: "Besides a report of an officer down, the worst radio call to get, the one that makes percussion drums sound off in your gut, is the report of a working house fire with children still inside screaming."

That very same reserve can send you laughing out loud: "In the movies, even the slightest cop knocks down a door in one kick. Real life is different. Once it took me twenty-seven tries. I know this because there was a sergeant next to me counting out loud encouragingly...If you show up at a call with a couple of other cops and you do have to kick down a door, you will subsequently have a brief discussion about who has to do it...One of you is maybe coming off back surgery so he's out. Another one kicked in the last door. Someone wore sneakers to work instead of boots...Sometimes you just make the newest guy boot it in. He's probably all jazzed up to do it anyway."

•

There's been countless books by cops, countless books about what it's like to be a cop, some fiction, some non-fiction, some straightforward informational. Were you worried about whether or not you still had anything to contribute to this ongoing conversation?

I'm still sort of worried about that. Writers with impressive credentials have already put out terrific books about cop life. Like *Blue Blood* by Edward Conlon, and *Homicide* by David Simon. But it seems most police books feature specialty units, like CSI or SVU. I don't think the general patrol perspective has always been as well-represented. I wanted to write about the kind of police officer the general public sees the most.

Also, cop fiction tends to present law enforcement in a way that is either overly sanitized (the police swoop in and save the day with plenty of yes sirs and no ma'ams), or far too bleak (chain-smoking cops sleep with witnesses and plant evidence). The reality, as is so often the case, is somewhere in-between. That's what I wanted to get across in writing this work. The in-between. As I say in the introduction to the book, sometimes the police are better than people think. Sometimes we're worse. Sometimes we're just different.

What made you pick the format you used?

My book started out as a traditional police memoir. I shopped it around a bit and was met with polite disinterest. Apparently the literary community didn't find me nearly as interesting as I found myself, which is always a bummer. So I mulled it over and figured what was important about my police experience wasn't necessarily my story, but the job of urban law enforcement itself. So I wrote a book about that with me standing in the background. I pop up now and again but I'm a bit of a sideshow. Which is as it should be. And the book ended up being sort of a cross between a reference book and some essays, sprinkled with arguably too many movie references.

Why 400 Things? Why not 401? 500? 300?

Initially there was no number in the title. It was called *Things Cops Should Know*. But my agent said people love lists, so he recommended I count up my passages and make it a nice even number. When I did the addition, it came out to something like four hundred and eight. Eight of the passages were, truth be told, pretty much filler anyway, so I cut them. And there's your four hundred.

Some of the pieces are extremely short, others long enough to qualify as an essay. Were you worried that the pieces weren't uniform? Did you ever have some sort of self-decided guideline about the length of the individual pieces?

I didn't sweat the lack of uniformity much. Some of the passages lent themselves to a more thorough treatment than others. No set guidelines — I just went with it. I liked that some of the pieces were short and punchy, like "Four minutes is about as long as someone can survive without a pulse." If I had maintained that same terse tone throughout the book, Chapter 15, #24 would begin and end with, "There exists a police code of silence." And the reader may have reasonably expected a bit more writerly unpacking of the subject than that.

The book is divided into categories. Did you have those in mind going in? Or did you write the pieces and come to the idea of organizing them by category later?

I had them in mind going in. I wanted to group my material so it didn't look like I was just randomly spewing police arcana on the page. As a cop, I seek out order and battle disorder. As a writer, I have the same mentality. I wanted an orderly book that hung together reasonably well. Hopefully I reached that goal.

There's an extremely deft tone exercised throughout the book: conversational yet polished, dry but not condescending, cynical but not so much so that it's immune to compassion. Yet whatever the underlying feeling in a piece — anger, poignancy, exasperation — the feelings are kept on a short leash, and the end result is a sense of — for lack of a better term — war-weariness. Did you have to work at that tone? Or was it something that came naturally because of your work?

Thanks. I'm not frequently associated with the word "deft." I don't know that I had to work at the tone much — if you put some time in as a cop in an urban area, the job does make you weary. Part of it is the constant exposure to toxic social conditions and seeing people at their hopeless worst.

You start out with fire in your belly. You're going to get out there and right wrongs and protect the weak and the innocent. And you get to do some of that. But a lot of the victories are minor and many of the frustrations are enduring and you soon learn that some of the innocent ain't all that innocent. You quickly start feeling like you're too old to change the world — even if you just turned, say, thirty.

You get coarsened by what you see — death and mayhem and awful things happening to decent people. You used to run and now you trudge. You still take motivation from the fact that there is meaning to the work even if there isn't always satisfaction. You do the job well because you still believe in right and wrong and that criminals need to be held accountable for the offenses they commit. And you adopt that detachment as a kind of protective shield.

It can actually be helpful in your investigations. Because you aren't, for instance, doing victims of violent crimes any favors by getting emotionally involved in their situation. You need distance and neutrality in order to be an objective fact-finder and bring their case to resolution. You need to look at things clearly and clinically. That is how you help those victims. That's how you honor them.

Although you created a non-narrative form, there is the sense of an underlying story although it works more like a mosaic than a narrative arc. One definitely gets a sense of the arc of your own experiences: youthful idealism and naiveté slowly giving way to accumulating experience and wisdom, and then that, in turn incorporating a cynicism. In other words, one feels a story rather than follows it. Were you aware of that in the writing? If not, do you see it now?

Well, even if I wasn't aware of that narrative arc, I'm now going to claim that's exactly what I was shooting for so I can sound like a better writer than I actually am. But the first draft of the book was largely stripped of feeling. It was about what cops do and what we see and didn't include much of our reactions to those things. An editor recommended I humanize the book more and try to place the reader in the cop's head. So I went back and retooled the chapters with that approach in mind. I think the book is stronger for it.

Anything else about your tactical approach to the book?

Every morning I would lie in an open coffin for a good hour or two before picking up a pen. Actually, that's not true. But poet John Donne used to do that. I think the earlier writers were a lot tougher than we are now.

PULP FICTION:
PRESERVING AN ICON
Max Allan Collins on Mickey Spillane

A week before he died in 2006, author Mickey Spillane turned to his wife and said, "When I'm gone, there's going to be a treasure hunt around here. Take everything you find and give it to Max – he'll know what to do."

"Max" is Max Allan Collins. He was, for a number of reasons, an ideal choice to be the keeper of the Spillane flame.

A fan of Spillane's since he'd been a kid, Collins had met the mystery writer at a convention in the early 1980s. The connection developed into both friendship and regular collaboration. But Collins was no junior partner in the duo.

Born in Muscatine, Iowa in 1948, he's been writing mysteries since he was a kid, eventually studying in the Iowa Writers' Workshop at the University of Iowa, one of the most renowned writing programs in the country.

By the late 1970s, Collins had published his first novel. Since then, he's published 49 more, another 17 movie or TV tie-in novels, and worked in almost every other literary format from comic strips to short stories to graphic novels and even to trading cards. His stature in his field is measured by his unmatched 16 Private Eye Writers of America Shamus nominations, as well as his regular nods from the Mystery Writers of America Edgar Awards.

Out of that enormous body of work, possibly his most recognized piece is the three-part graphic novel *Road to Perdition* on which he worked with illustrator Richard Piers Rayner, and which served as the basis for the acclaimed 2002 hit film directed by Sam Mendes, adapted by David Self, and starring Tom Hanks.

According to a 2002 interview, Collins' inspiration for *Perdition* was two-fold: "I'd been wanting to do something with the true story of (1930s crime boss) John Looney (the family name was changed to Rooney in the film) and his warped son Connor for a long, long time…" The other reason: "What made it an 'irresistible creative opportunity' was my need for work: I'd just been fired from the *(Dick) Tracy* strip…"

Perdition is moodier, more morally complex, and more melancholic than Spillane's work, yet in it one can still see what made Collins and Spillane such kindred spirits, and Collins such a perfectly-matched collaborator. *Perdition*'s Michael Sullivan – a hit man on a relentless crusade for revenge against the man who'd murdered his wife and younger son, and against the father figure who has sheltered the killer who is his own son – is a direct descendant of Spillane's iconic private eye, Mike Hammer, an equally relentless, equally brutal dealer in rough justice (which, in Hammer novels, is often interchangeable with revenge).

Here, Max Allan Collins talks about carrying on Spillane's work, the mystery writer's place in the genre's pantheon of big name talents, and his own *Road to Perdition*.

When you say "Mickey Spillane," what are the characteristics of his work that, to you, are his trademarks? As a brand, what does "Mickey Spillane" mean?

Today, Mike Hammer probably personifies the traditional tough private eye. That flows not just from Mickey's books, but from the various Stacy Keach TV shows. In the last century — you know, the 20th Century — Mickey Spillane was the epitome of sex and violence in crime fiction. Mike Hammer novels were "dirty books" in the 1950s and even early '60s.

The actual characteristics of his work are not so simplistic. Hammer is a combat veteran unhappy with the postwar world, a guy who values friendship in the way one G.I. in a foxhole values his buddy. As a hero, he was the first really dark protagonist, a tough, remorseless man who uses the bad guy's methods against the bad guys — the first hero to execute a villain, not turn that villain over to the authorities. Hammer is also the first private eye to sleep around with the lovely, willing women he meets. James Bond is only one of the other characters who would not have happened if Spillane hadn't shown the way.

What gets lost (in talking about his work) is Spillane's storytelling, which can be hypnotic — he is particularly good at arresting openings and shocking, surprising conclusions — and his *noir* poetry (is) a kind of surrealistic fever dream.

How did you and Mickey Spillane hook up?

Spillane was my obsession as an adolescent. I had discovered him and Hammett and Chandler about the same time, loved them all, but was dismayed to learn that Mickey did not share the critical praise heaped on the other two; that in fact he was blamed for all kinds of social ills from causing juvenile delinquency to lowering the standards of reading tastes. Before my career got off the ground, and after as well, I was his defender in articles and letters of comment. So, when the 1981 Bouchercon, in Milwaukee, needed a liaison between the con and Mickey, who was one of their guests of honor, I was asked.

Mickey and I hit it off, and did a memorable two-man panel at the con, which was his first appearance at such an event. He had the mistaken idea that he might not be greeted warmly by mystery fans, since a lot of his fellow mystery writers had been vicious in their criticism of him. Anyway, we became friends and I was one of his writer pals since Murrell's Inlet, South Carolina (where Spillane lived), wasn't exactly a writers' commune.

I visited his home once a year or so, and we began doing projects together — co-editing anthologies, creating a comic book, doing a number of movie projects, including my documentary about him, "Mike Hammer's Mickey Spillane," which you can find on the Criterion DVD and Blu-ray of *Kiss Me Deadly*.

How did you come to pick up the baton on the Spillane novels?

Mickey asked me to complete *The Goliath Bone* if necessary, which was the book he was working on when he became ill. He asked his wife, Jane, to have me complete the various other unfinished works, and she asked me to, and, of course, I said yes to all of that. Mickey was my hero as a kid, and I was a defender of his in my early career — he was, and is, very controversial — and we'd become friends in the early '80s. We did numerous projects together, anthologies, comic books, films.

Is Lady, Go Die! *the first Spillane novel you've completed?*

There were six substantial Hammer unfinished novel manuscripts. I did *The Goliath Bone, The Big Bang,* and *Kiss Her Goodbye* for Otto Penzler's line at Harcourt. This second round of three novels is being done for Titan, who I feel have a real grasp of popular culture and an unusual sense of history, for a publisher.

How incomplete was the manuscript? Any idea why Spillane never finished the book/didn't submit it for publication?

This was by far the earliest unfinished manuscript, dating to 1945, and with references in the text that made it clear it was the sequel to the first, hugely famous and popular *I, the Jury* (1947). The next earliest of the unfinished novels was *The Big Bang,* which dated to around 1965. So, this was a major find. But it was the shortest of the substantial manuscripts at around 80 pages. I found a single chapter from a later unfinished book with a similar theme, a similar set of crimes, and was able to use that as well, bringing the Spillane content up to match that of the other novels.

As to why he didn't finish it, I have two theories. One is that *I, the Jury* didn't sell well in hardcover — it didn't become a blockbuster till it hit paperback — and so he decided not to pursue a sequel.

The other is that he may have gone too far (in *Lady, Go Die!*) with the relationship between Mike Hammer and his secretary, Velda, and decided to back off. Spillane always wrestled with the love between Hammer and Velda because readers expected Hammer to be a randy guy bedding all sorts of "dames," but also would resent him if he betrayed the love of his life.

You have your own credits. Is it hard to suppress your own creative voice to pick up Spillane's? Did you ever find yourself being moved to take the story a certain way, but then holding yourself back because you realized that was more Max Allan Collins than Mickey Spillane?

I immerse myself in Mickey's work, reading and re-reading and marking up the several novels adjacent in time to the manuscript I'm completing. Initially, of course, I am working inside Mickey's manuscript, expanding and extending it, weaving my own stuff in, but staying faithful to the character, the tone, the style. By the time I run out of Spillane material, I'm fully absorbed in the voice of that book and it's really no problem.

Stylistically, I do watch myself in a couple of areas — Mickey's sentences tend to be simpler than mine, unless he's writing a stream-of-conscious passage, and he rarely uses semicolons, and I use a lot of those. Also, our sense of humor is different. Mine is sarcastic, his is more of a macho, Howard Hawks kind of dialogue. So I keep an eye on that.

Your original, Road to Perdition, *has a brooding melancholy quality which seems 180 degrees away from the more visceral, hard-boiled quality of Spillane. How much of a reach for you was it – at least initially – to go from something like* Perdition *to pick up Spillane's voice?*

Every story has its appropriate tone and voice. I just try to do what's appropriate for the story at hand. Moving from one thing to another – say, first-person to third-person — or from one form to another — say, graphic novel to novel — really is a positive thing, keeps me fresh and enthusiastic. So I'd say it's not a reach at all.

When you pick up Lady *or any of your other collaborations now, can you see where Spillane ends and Max Collins begins? Or is it a seamless melding?*

That's for others to say, but, again, I don't pick up where Spillane ends. I collaborate with him. I turn his 100 pages into 200 or more pages before I take over, and sometimes even then I've held back material of his to use later in the book.

In *Lady, Go Die!*, Velda gets kidnapped at the end of Spillane's fourth chapter. I held that back till much, much later in the book. In fact, I think that's another reason he may have put the manuscript aside — he realized he had gotten Velda kidnapped too early. Mike can't go on his rampage at the end of Chapter Four — that doesn't come till around Chapter Eleven.

It's been over a half-century since the peak of the popularity of the Mike Hammer novels, yet people are obviously still reading them. What is it about the books which still engages an audience?

The books have enormous energy, and Hammer is one of the great first-person voices in mystery fiction. Only Philip Marlowe and Archie Goodwin (narrator of Rex Stout's Nero Wolfe mysteries) equal him, I think. The emotional content is still surprisingly strong, and, despite a passage of time that includes (the work of) everybody from Sam Peckinpah to John Woo, Spillane's violence is still shocking, really powerful.

Do you think it's a fair appraisal that Spillane was a better storyteller than he was – from a literary point of view – a writer? Or do you think he's been short-changed by the critics?

Spillane has consistently been short-changed by critics. He was a born storyteller, but sometimes that term is used as a left-handed compliment.

Mickey was a writer who could do things that even Hammett and Chandler couldn't — his fever-dream prose was his own, and the strong emotional content was something very new to the mystery genre. He could construct better openings and opening sentences than anyone in the field, and his endings were astonishing. The first seven books,

written when he was a relatively young man, have a rough-hewn quality
— he was notorious for going with his first draft, just lightly edited —
but incredible passion and energy. His later books lack some of that,
but are much more polished, better-crafted. Early Spillane is primitive
genius. Later Spillane is polished professional.

Clearly, he belongs in the top tier of crime writers, certainly one of
the big three private eye writers: Hammett, Chandler, Spillane. Ross
Macdonald often is given Mickey's spot on that list, but Macdonald,
good as he was, was chiefly a Chandler imitator (and Chandler knew
it, and didn't like it). You might need to add Robert B. Parker to the
list of major private eye writers. I'm not a huge fan, but, like Mickey, he
changed the field and opened a door for the rest of us.

That's the frustrating thing to me — I understand that just because
Parker is not my cup of tea that doesn't mean he wasn't a major figure.
Those who dislike Mickey's work ignore the obvious impact he had on
mystery fiction and popular fiction in general, and really all of popular
culture. No James Bond without Mike Hammer, or Shaft or Dirty
Harry or Jack Bauer or Spencer's pal Hawk for that matter, and dozens
of other tough protagonists who take the law into their own hands and
buck the system.

*Consider the great literary and film/TV private eyes: Sherlock Holmes,
Nick Charles, Sam Spade, Philip Marlowe, Lew Archer, The* Rockford
Files' *Jim Rockford,* Chinatown's *J.J. Gittes – where does Mike Hammer
fit on that spectrum? Is there anything he shares with them? What is it that
distinguishes him; that makes Mike Hammer Mike Hammer?*

That's a great list. Hammer is the toughest, the randiest, and
probably the most famous. What all the private eyes share is a rugged
individualism, a distrust of the system, and a reliance on rough justice;
none rougher than Hammer.

*Are there more Mike Hammers coming? If you ever exhausted
Spillane's backlog, would you ever consider writing a Mike Hammer novel
from scratch as has been done with the James Bond novels?*

There are two more coming from Titan from substantial manuscripts – *Complex 90* and *King of the Weeds*. There are three more significant but shorter works — 40-page range — that I will complete if readers are interested. I doubt we'd go past that, but if we do, there are plenty of shorter fragments, including complete opening chapters, from non-Hammer Spillane stories that could be converted into Hammer yarns. There's no need for me to create anything from whole cloth.

This isn't about the market, to me. It's about getting Mickey's work out there in a finished form. Mickey only wrote 13 complete Hammer novels in his lifetime. Characters like Nero Wolfe, Hercule Poirot, and Perry Mason were in 75 or more. In the 1950s and early '60s, when Mickey was the bestselling mystery writer in the world — a position he held for decades — he had only written seven novels. So, finding Mike Hammer material, unpublished, in his files is a major find. And, for me, a major responsibility. Adding six books to the canon — and as these are co-written by Mickey and largely plotted by him, they are canon — is a big deal. At least it is to me.

GENRE INVERSION:
BLACK AND BLUE
Thomas E. Kennedy and His Non-Noir
Noir, *Beneath the Neon Egg*

If you turn a finely-cut diamond in the light, as each facet catches the beams it will throw off different colors. In his *Copenhagen Quartet*, award-winning author/essayist Thomas E. Kennedy turns the eponymous Danish capital in the light of the seasons, each novel set in a different part of the year, each volume a different face of the city casting a different light. In his latest and final installment in the quartet – *Beneath the Neon Egg* – that color is the icy bluish black of a Danish winter's night.

Patrick Bluett – "Blue" to his few friends – is a middle-aged American living in Copenhagen, earning his living as a translator, living a life incomplete, looking for something on the cold streets of nighttime Copenhagen to fill the empty spaces of his life

Kennedy's previous installment in the quartet – *Kerrigan in Copenhagen* – warm with the Danish spring, bubbled along with a bounce perfectly suited to the extended pub crawl of its often inebriated protagonist. But *Neon Egg* has a harder edge, Blue a more melancholy streak of disconnection, and his Copenhagen – a city which Kennedy, as always, etches in exquisite detail – radiates a more somber palette. It's there even in Bluett's name which Kennedy picked because of its association with *l'heure bleue* – the blue hour, that point in the twilight photographers refer to as "the sweet light."

One of my first reactions to the book was it had a noiry feel although it's hardly a book that fits the classic mold of a roman noir. I once told a writing class that they could go into an episode of any decent one-hour

105

drama and find all the basic elements for a great story. It was just that limited by the format of the series, by budget, shooting and running time constraints, regular commercial interruptions, and the need to appeal to a network audience, the best you were going to get out of those elements was good episodic TV. Beneath the Neon Egg *almost feels to me like someone similarly stripped out the basic elements from a noir – a femme fatale, the (relatively) good guy she leads to his destruction, the concerned friend who wants to get to the bottom of his death – and said, instead of pushing them down the suspense/mystery route, I'm going to take them someplace else. So, to me, the book reads like a literary work, but I still detect, in a lovely way, these echoes of noir. Are you aware of that? Were you conscious of that going in, and if not, how do you respond to that idea now?*

Yes, I was as conscious of this as I ever am, but I am a firm adherent of what Wright Morris said which clarified process for me in the 1970s. Morris said, "How do I know what I want to say until I've said it?" My starting point with *Neon Egg* was that because winters are so dark in Copenhagen (in deep winter you get barely six hours of gloomy light a day), I thought that the seasonal celebration of winter in my *Copenhagen Quartet* should be noir, but with modifications. I didn't want the main plot line to be fixed; you have Bluett's post-divorce, wandering search for love (paralleled with John Coltrane's *A Love Supreme*, which is essentially a search for divine love *a la* Dante's *The Divine Comedy)*, and parallel with that (Bluett's friend) Sam's exploring the dark side of his sexual passion (which is maybe another, narcissistic aspect of the same thing). And I didn't want the villains to be punished or the "crime" to be "solved." Your take on it is so (flatteringly, I might say) right. It's a roman noir but also attempts to be a literary novel (whatever that is!).

One reviewer said it is a literary fiction and pulp fiction laid side by side – though I object to the "pulp fiction" label. I take it that reviewer was referring to Sam's story as pulp fiction, but I believe Sam's story could just as well be literary fiction.

I think a couple of the reviewers of *Neon Egg* were perplexed, or even embarrassed, by the fact that Bluett is revealed in the mundane details of his thought processes, but a number of our thoughts *are* quite ordinary. The Danish-Czech novelist Per Smidl said about *Neon Egg* that those thought processes embarrass some people (and some reviewers) because they are subject to those same thoughts themselves and they don't want to let on that they think those things – or are not aware of it. I like that.

Along with those elements, there were others I felt contributed to that noiry feel. By my page count, somewhere around one-third of the novel takes place at night, or as the day is fading, and once the sun goes down Copenhagen becomes a different place. Was this by design? The dangerous things – and the sense that dangerous things might happen – only seem to occur after dark. Again: was this a conscious choice or did the story develop organically that way?

I refer once again to my Wright Morris quote – it was a mix of conscious plan and developing organically. One of the things that inspired me to set it largely at night was a sign that I discovered one night, a simple brass plaque, on a wall by a door in central Copenhagen that said simply, "The Velvet Room/10 pm to 4 am/ Ring Bell." As it was just 10 pm, I rang the bell, and an attractive, middle-aged woman opened the door, and she said, "Yes?" And I said, "May I come in?" And she opened the door wider and I entered a very strange place. This, of course, was the model for The Satin Room in *Neon Egg* – which I transplanted to the other side of town for fear of lawsuits (though it now has been replaced by an Irish pub!).

The first time I went in there, I was the first customer and sat at the bar and ordered a double vodka which cost about fifty bucks, but then a beautiful woman came out, all alone, onto the dance floor and danced for me to a song by Prince, and she took all of her clothes off and wound up about a foot from me where I sat at the bar and whipped her long dark hair so it slashed across my face. Then she disappeared as quickly as she had appeared.

Another time a Swedish millionaire visited me, and he asked me to show him the wild side of Copenhagen, and I took him into The Velvet Room, and he was immediately surrounded by three or four gorgeous

Brazilian ladies of the night – then my task was to get him *out* of there fast. The Swede thought the hookers *liked* him, but it was clear that they could smell his millions on him from when he walked in the door.

In The Velvet Room I never had any hint of violence but you scratch the surface of a sleek place like that and you find something raw beneath the surface of pleasure. That was part of what inspired me to develop the story of *Neon Egg* in that direction. After all, a neon egg is a symbol of a natural thing that is artificial.

Further, I have never experienced any violence in Copenhagen, but I read about it in the papers. For example, one time on New Year's Eve I was about a block away at the same time as a guy my own age, also a family father, was knifed down by a young man. I also read about the episode that Bluett and Liselotte witness in the novel: five guys stomping a guy outside of Christiania in the wee hours of a winter night.

But things happen in the summer morning, too. One summer morning at about 8 a.m., I was waiting for a bus to visit my son in the hospital. Directly across the street from me was an all-night bar, right on the banks of Black Dam Lake, and as I was waiting, the doors opened and out of the bar stepped three young people: a young girl and two guys. They walked directly across the street to me, so I busied myself reading the bus schedule, thinking that I was in danger of being kicked to an invalid. The young woman came up behind me and draped herself across my back and asked what bus I was looking for. The two young men were studying me. I thought of offering them some money for more drink, which was no doubt what they were after, but I said, truthfully, "I'm looking for the bus to the hospital. My son is hospitalized and I'm going to visit him." Immediately, the two young men straightened up and bowed in the European fashion, and one of them said ruefully, "I am very sorry to hear that," and the three drifted off along the lake in the summer morning.

Melancholy is a hard thing to pull off without overdoing it and becoming drippingly melodramatic. There's a certain subtle flavor of unhappy ennui which bubbles up deep into **Beneath the Neon Egg** *which was right on the money I thought. It seems to come out of a combination* *of all that darkness and the short days, the cold, the fact that Bluett works at home in isolation. Those passages where the reader follows him through all those minor activities – cleaning the apartment, a little exercise, etc. – made me think of a long-term prisoner trying to fill the days in a long sentence. Like many noir protagonists, Bluett is an outsider, although not in the classic noir mold (Mitchum was never going to play Bluett), but he's just as disconnected from a lot of the world around him as any of the demimonde anti-heroes of classic noir. Comment?*

That's a great take on it! I hadn't thought of it that way, but Bluett is in a kind of prison cell of loneliness. And you're right; Mitchum will never play Bluett. As much as I admire Mitchum, I didn't want to create a character that was a tough guy. I always marvel how Bogart knocks a guy out with a short left jab. In truth, you've got to be Mike Tyson to knock a guy out and he uses a pounding right. The nicest compliment I ever got on my prose is by the poet-football player (for SMU) who was a finalist for the National Book Award for Poetry last year and who said, "Your work is a Tyson upper-cut in the world of contemporary fiction – thanks for knocking me out." (Thought I'd just slip in a little advertisement for myself there!)

Anyway, my noir character is not a tough cat – he is a wanderer in Copenhagen nights and makes himself scarce when there's a barroom fight. He's only too aware of the fact of his vulnerability.

The lake reminds me of the oil spill in Ross Macdonald's The Drowning Pool. Pool *is one of Macdonald's Lew Archer novels, and during its opening pages, there's a background incident; an offshore oil well begins spewing oil into the ocean off southern California. The well happens to belong to the family Archer is hired to work with. As he digs deeper and the shit piles higher over the course of the novel, that oil spill gets wider and more damaging. Bluett's world is cold, only ever briefly sunlit, he hungers for connection but is often isolated, and through all of that the lake is hard, cold, and dark. Toward the end of the novel when Bluett begins to thaw himself, so does that great, dark lake. Did you just get lucky or was this part of the planned architecture of the novel?*

That's a fine take on the lake. I read all those noir novels in the 1970s – Hammet and Chandler and George V. Higgins and Ross Macdonald and Ed McBain, et al. And I have always been attracted by the Copenhagen street lakes – among other reasons because they're natural lakes, formed by glaciers in the ice age – and in 1996 when I got divorced, I got lucky in buying a condominium on Black Dam Lake. I sold it seven years later and have been kicking myself in the pants ever since. But part of the reason I used that setting is because there's an Irma supermarket neon sign on the wall across the lake of a neon chicken laying neon eggs and because there is an expression in Danish which says, "I'll go out to Black Dam Lake (Sortedamsø)," which means, "Goodbye, cruel world." The first year I moved into that apartment that winter the lake froze. I used to walk across the lake to a café on the other side.

And all along I wanted to parallel the four parts of the novel with the four parts of John Coltrane's *A Love Supreme*. That jazz symphony begins formally, then goes into a psalm (which is very much like a Gregorian chant of the group members chanting, "A love supreme," over and over), then goes into a kind of bop or post-bop wildness that approaches a pure vibration of sound. I asked myself how I could represent that pure vibration in language. I considered doing it in language, in alphabetical form – like Kerouac's imitations of the sound of the surf at Big Sur. But I actually never liked reading that. I'm sure Kerouac can read it aloud and bring it to life, but the letters are just dead on the page, I think – *slurp slurp slurp splash*… Then I got the idea that I could represent it symbolically. The lake is frozen all through the novel, and in the end – when Bluett begins to find his way to a supreme love, in Dante's words, "But my volition now, and my desires,/were moved like a wheel revolving evenly/By love that moves the sun and starry fires." — the hard icy water begins to melt.

One aspect of the novel that is almost pure noir – to the point where even most noirs don't have the nerve to go there – is how the plot ultimately plays out. It defies the (a presumption on my part) reader's desire for some sort of justice or revenge; the bad guys get away with having destroyed

Bluett's friend and gutting his estate, Bluett destroys the evidence of his friend's kink. The ending denies catharsis, but at the same time that's what makes it feel honest. You had to know it would probably piss at least some readers off, but you went that route anyway?

Yes, I don't know if I had the idea when I started writing it, but I realized that if I were to break the formula, I had to deny myself justice or vengeance on the Russian bitch. Let them choke on their profits, Bluett thinks at last. Let them live choking. He is concerned that he failed his friend, that he should have insisted that Sam open up to him when he visited him that last time and when Bluett can see his eyes are in despair.

This is part of the search for love, I think; in order to let the material goods go and regret the fact that you are not living up to love. I'll never forget the eyes of a friend who one day said goodbye to me for the last time – he knew it, I knew it. I was speechless. It was haunting, the expression in his eyes.

Despite that, the book ends on a hopeful note. Bluett seems on his way to making an honest reconnection with his son and daughter, and he reaches out to Liselette. The book generally doesn't feel optimistic, but then there's this ending and it vaguely resembles an aspect of Kerrigan in Copenhagen's *finish. Are you a secret romantic?*

No secret about it. One reviewer complained that all four novels of the *Copenhagen Quartet* end happily! Give me a break! But at what cost? Someone complained that even Voss (whose name I picked because it sounds very much like *fos* in Danish which means a "losing card) in *Falling Sideways* (the 2011 second installment in the quartet) ends happily – I don't see that; all four may end on a more or less "up" moment, but all the personas still have to face the limitations of their characters and what the world and circumstances have made of them. The one has been tortured and has lost his wife and son, the one still has her daughter who killed herself, Voss is still effed up, Michela's mother is still in her mental twilight, Breathwaite is still bankrupt, his son still catches himself in his naked carelessness. I think that Bluett will bear the weight of his failure with his friend Sam, it will haunt him all the rest of his life, even if he is approaching love. And they still have to die. As Sophocles says, "Count no man happy until he is laid in his grave." A supreme irony!

WRITERS ON WRITING:
A WRITER'S REBOOT

She saw me coming up the walk and even before I got to the open front door, she'd burst out of the lobby; a short, cherubesque middle-aged woman, inexhaustibly bubbly and all smiles.

"Is this it?" I asked.

"You're here for the residency?"

I nodded.

She scooped up my hand in hers and started pulling/guiding me through the lobby. "Welcome, welcome! I'm Renee!" – I would later learn this was poet Renee Ashley – "Let's get you checked in!" I was tugged into a little, cluttered office off the lobby. "Let's get this boy a room!"

This boy.

After weeks of building nervousness, I thought this was a good sign, a *great* sign, a vanity-feeding great sign. *This boy.* She didn't say, "This *man,*" or even, "This *guy.*" *This boy.* I felt ten years lighter and could've kissed her because of it.   Hard.

Then the college kid doing the check-in put my dick in the dirt when he gave me a quick glance and asked, "Student or faculty?"

Which told me my barber hadn't quite trimmed as much gray off my head as I'd hoped when I'd been sitting in his chair two days earlier. *Or faculty.* I could hear what was left of my grays stand up on my head and crack, "You ain't foolin' anybody, pallie."

"Student."

I cannot tell you how funny that word felt in my mouth. *Student.* Except for a warm-up class I'd taken at Rutgers the previous spring, I hadn't been on a campus as a student in decades. Yeah, you read that right: *decades.*

I was a month shy of turning 58. The number doesn't make you feel old. The fact that you can say "It's been decades..." about so damn much of your life sits on you heavier than your aching joints, bad back, and blurry eyes.

As I started hauling my gear out of my car, I saw other cars pulling up in the parking lot and I saw dads – seems like it's always dads — helping sons and daughters carry *their* gear inside. There's one image still sticks with me: a thick-in-the-middle, balding dad loaded down with bags, and his smaller, scrawnier kid with more bags and a guitar strapped to his back, the two of them wrestling their way through a side door. It was the guitar that did it; that just seemed so...*college*. As one student after another came waddling in laden with their stuff, it was those little accoutrements – the small desktop fan, the flex necked desk lamp, that kid's guitar – hanging out of their respective piles that brought it home to me: *college!*

I started having flashbacks, 40 years earlier, stepping out of my mother's car into killer Carolina heat, in front of a dingy-looking dorm, my mom behind me noodging, "Ask someone where we go!" and me, scared, first time away from home, dressed nice as they used to say, forcing myself to go up to this barefooted, bell-bottomed guy with long, scraggly hair sitting on the veranda strumming a guitar. I felt like I'd been dropped on another planet and was wondering if I wasn't stuck in the biggest mistake of my life.

Standing in the open door of my dorm suite a couple of lifetimes later, it hit me again: you're a 57-year-old college student...in a dorm... with a roomie. I hadn't shared living quarters with someone I wasn't boinking in – you guessed it – decades.

It was hard, at that point, not to have the old fear come back; you know, the one about biggest mistake etc.

But there was never – never had been – a question of backing out. Necessity, I'd learned by that point, had become the mother of reinvention.

Four years before, I'd been given the boot from Home Box Office where I'd had a rather cushy 9-to-5 home for 27 years. Toward the end, they had belatedly become aware they were paying me a good dollar to sit in my office watching YouTube videos and occasionally work on my Not-So-Great American Novel. I'd become obsolete, and since I only knew how to do a job they no longer needed me to do, they adjudged it was time for me to – in the corporate lexicon of the day – "seek other opportunities."

They were very gracious and generous, more so than, on reflection, I probably deserved. Still, after being that long in the same place – and particularly when the subsequent months proved middle-aged corporate guys who only know how to do one obsolete thing are pretty much screwed in the job market – for all HBO's graciousness and generosity, getting shown the door still felt like a double traumatic amputation by wood chipper topped off with a kick in the nuts. You can't breathe and you know you're going to have to learn to walk all over again in an entirely new way on your sore, bloody stumps.

The thing people like to say at a time like that – and my HBO bosses said it and my wife said it and my friends said it – is, "You'll look back on this and see this was the best thing that ever happened to you."

I think a lot of people say that so they won't feel bad that you just lost your meal ticket, and God knows certainly at the time nothing felt "best thing" about it (remember: amputation, wood chipper, kick in the nuts).

But even if some of them didn't mean it, or were just saying it trying to make me feel better, or make themselves feel better, here's the thing: damned if it didn't turn out to be true.

Back in the early 1990s, I'd gone for my Master's in Communications at Montclair State. Somebody from the program remembered me and invited me to come back after I'd graduated to teach a course about cable television. I thought it might be fun to see what the whole teaching thing was about, although, frankly, the main reason I said yes was mercenary: it was a way to pick up a few extra bucks.

About two weeks into the course, I was in love with teaching, enough so that I knew that sooner or later, this was something I wanted to do as a second career. HBO made it a lot sooner than the later I'd hoped for, and it took me a year of knocking my head against closed corporate doors to realize I was done with corporate (actually, it was more like corporate was done with me), but then my wife – as she tends to do – threw a little common sense into the mix.

"You always wanted to teach," she said. "Seems like this is the time to do it."

Almost exactly a year after I'd left HBO, I got my first teaching gig, and I've been more-or-less teaching steadily since as an adjunct at several Jersey universities and colleges. Adjunct pay can't support a gerbil, and there are times I have students – even whole classes – I want to go after with a fungo bat and club like baby seals. But for all that, I've never done anything as fulfilling, as *fun* as teaching.

When you're standing at the front of the class, doing what you're there to do, you can tell from one moment to the next whether you've hooked your students or not. When you do – and you don't always – but when you do, when you see they're engaged, when you see something's coming back from the class in response to what you're putting out, that's a buzz nothing else I've done has ever given me, including my writing.

You write – a book, a play, a movie – you're not at the other end, you don't see how it works with the audience. Oh, you get to see reviews (and I've had my share of good with some choice not-so-goods thrown in to keep me humble), and they're always nice to read, but it's not the same thing. In a classroom, you *know* – instantly, immediately – if you've connected.

And then, when you see what I hear some teachers refer to as the a-*ha!* moment light up in your students' eyes, well, pallie, you've just taught – as the saying goes – someone to fish, and let me tell you, there's not a bigger rush than that.

The hitch was that in my state, New Jersey, you're not eligible for fulltime employment as a college instructor unless you have what's referred to as a "terminal degree." For most fields of study, that's a PhD, and with kids coming up on college age, a mortgage, and an adjunct's pay, there was no way I could pull that off.

But in some of the creative fields, an MFA is accepted as a terminal degree. Two-three years? That I could do.

There are three universities in New Jersey which offer a Creative Writing Master of Fine Arts degree: Rutgers and William Paterson, which are state universities, and Fairleigh Dickinson, which is a private school.

I applied to Rutgers in the unforgivable arrogance that as selective as their program was – they take only 10 new students each fall — I was a shoo-in. Hey, I had eight published books under my belt, another due in a few months, and one in the pipeline, plus a couple of movies (most small, most crappy, but still…) and some stage work. My letters of recommendation included one from a five-time Emmy-winner. How could I lose?

Like this: they say no. I don't know why – Rutgers doesn't explain – but after I spent a day crying about it, I looked up the requirements for Fairleigh and William Paterson and quickly banged out applications for both.

Maybe karma recognized that the Rutgers rejection had left me suitably chastened and humbled and figured I deserved a treat; both schools accepted me.

Trying to weigh the pros and cons of each, money was not an inconsiderable factor (remember? Adjunct pay? Can't feed a gerbil?). As a state school, William Paterson was cheaper, and both schools – according to my online poking around – were rather highly rated.

But the program at William Paterson was a traditionally-structured one, while FDU's was a low-residency program, meaning I wouldn't have to be on campus for most of its run which, in turn, meant I could still work and keep some gerbil-grade money coming in (starving gerbil or not, adjuncting and the occasional freelance gig provide my only income).

And there was this. The FDU program had been designed for writers, its faculty were all published writers (I googled them all). It was going to be writers teaching writers in a way that writers thought would work for writers. William Paterson's program is a more conventionally academic program; writing courses mixed with prerequisites such as 12 credits in lit study. In fact, their program is labeled an MFA in Creative and Professional Writing. I'd argue – with all respect to WPU – that the William Paterson program is more about equipping people to teach (requirements also include three credits for a "teaching portion"), while the FDU program is about helping wannabe writers become writers

All that in mind, despite the extra cost, I thought the FDU program would be the better fit.

FDU'S MFA doesn't work in semesters but in 10-week modules running back to back in the spring and fall. Between those pairs of modules, there are residencies: intense 10-day sprints of workshops, lectures, practicums, and readings to ground you in the program and get you charged up for the modules where your work is handled through email and other online pipelines.

The residencies are just that: you reside at the campus (actually, if you're in-state, you can commute if you want). You spend the 10 days in a dorm. With a roomie. Just like a college kid.

(Point of clarification: the residencies alternate between FDU's Madison campus in August, and Wroxton, England in January. I heard about Wroxton and I got to thinking there were a lot of pockets on campus a hell of a lot deeper than mine.

While the semester tuition covers the residencies, rooms, most meals, it doesn't cover transportation or off-campus expenses. The Wroxton trip isn't mandatory, thank God. Even if I could cover the cost, no way I could look my wife in the eye after New Year's and say, "Sorry, love, off to England to do the writer thing, have fun with the kids; ta!" Wherever you spend them, three residences are required as part of the path to graduation.)

And as you may have divined from my opening paragraphs, the whole dorm thing made me a bit nervous. I had visions of being stuck with a 24-year-old lit nerd asking Mr. Mesce if he knew where he could score good weed.

As an older student, I had other concerns as well. I wasn't comfortable about leaving my wife to deal with our two daughters while holding down a fulltime job while I was off on a writer's holiday (ok, a writer's working vacation, but still, it wasn't like breaking rocks which is still easier than wrangling two teenaged girls), but she's a good one she is, and said, "You're going. We'll be alright" (actually, I thought she seemed too damned sure they'd be fine without me and even seemed a little eager to push me out the door).

The school's main campus – and the site of the residency – is in Madison. The school is situated on what had, at one time, been an estate belonging to the Twombleys/Vanderbilts (yeah, *those* Vanderbilts), with grounds sculpted by the legendary Frederick Olmstead of New York's Central Park fame. One of the school's main buildings – and the place where MFA residents would do most of their work – was in what had once been the family mansion.

The dorm – a kind of faux Federal style thing – was a lot nicer than the dump I'd lived in as an undergrad in South Carolina ("Don't step on the cockroaches; it only pisses them off and then they come back with their friends to beat the crap out of you").

In front of the dorm, in what would have been a painfully obvious symbol if I'd made it up, the road by the campus was getting repaved (get it? Like I was "repaving" my life for a fresh start? Don't wince; like I said, I didn't make it up).

So, there I was, standing in the doorway to my dorm suite, biggest mistake etc. I'd read the books we'd been assigned as prep reading before the residency: National Book Award-winning poet Jean Valentine's collection, *Door in the Mountain;* Guggenheim fellow Sam Lipsyte's short story collection *The Fun Parts;* Pulitzer Prize finalist Lydia Millet's *Magnificence; The New Yorker* staff writer James Wood's *How Fiction Works;* and a couple of issues of *TLR*, the school's literary magazine.

This was serious stuff. Literature. The Real Deal.

And that wasn't me. Look, I'm no artist. At best, I'm a decent storyteller, a not awful entertainer. There's a scene in the movie *Barton Fink* (1991) that always struck a resonant chord with me. Young, idealistic, artistically ambitious/pretentious playwright Barton is spouting off to a veteran writer about how he finds his writing comes from some deep inner pain and blah blah blah.

To which the vet replies, "Me, I just enjoy making things up."

I hadn't told anybody at FDU I was published. After the Rutgers debacle, I wondered if maybe I hadn't bragged *too* much; that maybe they thought some young blood on the way up could benefit more from their program than I could. I don't *know* this, but I felt it.

FDU doesn't require a resume or transcripts or recommendations when you apply for their Creative Writing MFA; the decision to accept or pass on you is based simply, solely on a writing sample. You cut it or blow it on your ability (which makes an acceptance quite a writing honor in itself). I didn't have to tell anybody what I'd done, so I didn't.

And there's this. I wanted to go into the program on an even footing with everyone else there. I didn't want anybody thinking *I* thought I was something special, that I had some special insights, that I was *Da Man!*

Because I wasn't. I'd gotten some stuff done, sure, but it's not like you heard me on NPR shilling my latest release or getting reviewed in *The New York Times Literary Review.* I hadn't had a significant commercial release in 10 years (and that had been a marketplace dud), and with each year since then it seemed all the more sure my commercial writing career was, if not completely flat-lined, at the very least gasping its last breaths. The most generous way you could describe my status as a professional writer would be as a little-noted if critically respectable flop. I didn't want to go into the FDU program as a writer; I wanted to go in there as a student.

An anxious, am-I-out-of-my-league, mid-life-doubting student.

FRIDAY

My roomie showed up later that afternoon and it demonstrated FDU shrewdness in how they pair up their residency residents. No where's-the-good-weed kid. Jeff had been a rock 'n' roll journalist at 18 back in the 1980s (and didn't name-drop unless pushed), burned out on "the whole celebrity journalism thing" after some years globe-trotting, got into real estate flipping before getting clobbered in the crash of the late '00s, and had his hands in a few pies to keep going financially. He was married, had two kids (girls, like me, though considerably younger, and which he doted on – him on the phone overheard through his bedroom door: "You lost *another* tooth? That's two in two days! Are you sure you're not knocking them out on purpose?"), had to hustle to keep the bucks coming in, so we had enough in common to close the gap, and enough differences to make the pairing interesting.

And, by the way, maybe I hit the dorm/roomie thing too hard. The upper classmen dorm where FDU houses residency attendees is made up of suites: separate bedrooms, each with an attached bathroom, sharing a kitchen and common room (it was nicer than my first post-grad apartment and about the same size). During the regular year, these suites are supposed to house four people in which case it probably feels a little *Das Boot*-ish, but one person to a bedroom? Works quite nicely.

The first day is mostly schmoozing: check-in, unload and get settled, meet the roomie, and then a reception dinner at The Mansion where we were introduced to Rene Steinke, a National Book Award finalist who had recently taken over direction of FDU's Creative Writing program. There was a reading after dinner where we were treated to the work of one of the faculty, prize-winning poet David Daniel.

If your idea of poets is some weedy, overly-serious, reality-detached artsy-fartsy type, Daniel quickly disabuses you of such prejudices. Daniel, too, is aware of the preconception. He told a story of being in Boston some years ago and wanting a remembrance from The Commons during a dig where the city was replacing/expanding the underground garage there. His wanting a piece of the old garage had something to do with a poem Daniel liked. Daniel went up to one of the construction workers and, wary of the reception he might get by telling the guy he was a poet, instead, lied and told him his father had been a construction worker who'd worked on the original garage. He immediately felt guilty because the worker suddenly warmed to him.

"What section did he work on?" the guy asked him.

"Oh, well, ya know, I don't really remember," Daniel mumbled.

Then, even more guilt when the guy gave him a brick and said, "Tell your father this came from Section Such-and-Such. He'll know."

A burly, often T-shirted guy who looks like he'd be at home in a neighborhood saloon pounding down the Budweiser, David Daniel's a gregarious, funny, and talented writer who got me – definitely not a poetry guy – enjoying his poetry.

I had decided – so my family didn't get the impression I was happy to be out of the house – to commute over the weekend, so after the reading ended around eight, I took the 45-minute ride home, briefly caught up with my family and then crashed on the sofa to watch some TV (unless you bring one, there's no TVs in the dorm; come to think of it, I didn't see one anywhere on campus).

SATURDAY

I was up at seven, walked our dog, had breakfast (the residency provides lunches and dinners, but you're on your own for breakfast), then jumped in the car and headed back up to Madison for a 9:45 informational meeting with complimentary bagels (I noticed over the course of the residency, that new writers – apparently quickly learning the veteran's paranoia of never knowing where their next meal is coming from and/or making sure they get their tuition's worth – didn't leave many leftovers at these all-you-can-eats) where Rene Steinke walked us briskly through residency do's and don't's. This dove-tailed with a two-hour orientation for newbies explaining how both the residency and the program as a whole operated.

The orientation was followed by a two-hour lunch period which gives you some breathing time, and then things started getting serious.

The afternoon kicked off with a "generative workshop" led by Rebecca Chace (her memoir *Chautaqua Summer* had been an "Editor's Choice" and "Notable Book" in *The New York Times)* entitled "Fragments: Break the Rules for Rhythm and Subtext." We took a hard look at how Joshua Ferris' *The New Yorker* short story, "The Fragments," worked.

Ferris' had complemented his main story of a relationship going down the toilet with a mosaic of overheard real-life conversation snippets he'd picked up on the streets of New York.

Chace's exercise for us was to find what she called the "moment of exhilaration" for each of us in the story, which I took to mean that moment when something in us responded with a "Wow!," an "Ouch!," a BOOM! etc. There was something a little elementary about it, but it was still enlightening, and the exuberant Chace made it fun.

That 90-minute session was followed with a one-hour interview/Q & A with Jean Valentine, hosted by David Daniel, on her experiences translating the poetry of Russian poet Marina Tsvetaeva *(Dark Elderberry*

Branch: Poems of Marina Tsvetaeva) who'd been writing in the early part of the 20th Century. The essence of the discussion was that, in translation, the best one can hope for is an approximation; translation is always, said Valentine, "a compromise."

Quote of the night from Valentine when asked what – since a word-for-word translation wouldn't do justice to the poet's intent – she set as her target, she replied, as if the original poet was still alive, "What *she* could live with."

That led to dinner after which there were some student readings enough of which were impressive to the degree that if I had been 30 self-doubting years younger, I'd have probably thrown up my hands declaring, "I'm done!" and walk out of the program. I won't say they were all superlative – because they weren't – but in each case it was clear why they'd been accepted into the program.

Then followed Jean Valentine, again, this time reading from her own work.

Ms. Valentine is a small chip of a woman, with loose gray hair prone to fall down over her face. But she was the perfect instrument for reading her poetry: a delicate woman speaking in a small, but clear, equally delicate voice, delicately rendering delicate verse.

Like I said: I'm not a poetry guy. Nothing against it, but my brain just doesn't work that way. I don't know what makes good poetry good. But this slip of a lady, with her quiet, gentle reading had me enraptured.

Back home again, more hurried smooches, "Daddy we miss you!," "I miss you, too!", almost falling asleep on the sofa in front of the TV, breakfast, walk the dog and back up to Madison.

SUNDAY

The morning was given over to a workshop. Students are grouped with a mentor for their modules, and the residencies are the only time the entire group and mentor sit together face to face. My first module mentor was Walter Cummins whose publishing track record includes memoirs, essays, novels, and over 100 short stories many of which have been gathered into five published collections. Cummins is a down-topped gentleman with a properly literary Hemingway beard, but thankfully lacking Hemingway's overbearing jerkdom. Instead, he was a supportive, gentle – yet critical – guide to our finding our way around or through the missteps we'd made in our submissions.

The groups are small. One of the mentors had wound up in the hospital from a car accident the day before the residency had begun, so our group was rolled into hers and it still only totaled five students, ranging in age from *well*-into-middle-agedom (me) to a more typical post-grad mid-20s.

(At this point I'd be remiss if I didn't give props to the redoubtable and brilliant Ellen Akins – the unfortunate lady who'd gotten popped by a car at Newark airport. With a kamikaze-like commitment to her students, Ellen was emailing notes on her module students' work from her hospital bed, and by Sunday she was back on campus, arm in a sling, acting like her broken shoulder was nothing more than a mild inconvenience.)

I was a bit intimidated by the other members of the group not because I'd written what I thought was a bad piece (it was a decent piece of storytelling), but everyone else had, it was obvious to me, done work obviously inspired at least to some degree by personal experiences: death of a close friend by o.d., marriage in trouble, even the Y/A murder mystery set in a fast food joint drew on one writer's sister's experiences at a fried chicken place (I'd written a WW II bit).

If workshops are going to do anybody any good, you have to get over the natural hesitancy to criticize somebody's work to their face, and to do it without coming off like a smartass or know-it-all jerk. That hesitancy holds on harder when you feel you're going to be poking holes in something that obviously has a personal meaning to the writer (by the way, writers: "But it really happened that way" doesn't alibi truth-inspired fiction that doesn't work). Discussing the first piece – a generally strong item about a young man losing his best friend to drugs — it looked like *nobody* was going to say anything bad.

I girded my loins – which is what you do with your loins—and after two students had thrown softballs said, "I guess I'll make the first critical remarks."

"Good!" Cummins said, not in a malicious way, but because he needed the ice to be broken, and be broken by one of us instead of him so we'd all know it was ok to have a problem with a piece. If you're feeling sick, you don't get well by the doctor telling you, "Hey, that's a nice head of hair you got!" He has to tell you, "Stop eating so much crap." After the ice-breaking, the discussions grew increasingly free-flowing and productive.

It's hard for most writers – hell, it's hard for *any* writer – to get out of his or her own head and see a piece the way other people see it. You write a piece, you know what you want it to do, what you want things in it to mean, how you feel about it; you have all that so strongly in you, that there's always the danger your brain is drawing on that to spackle over holes on the page. Inside your head, you see the story you meant to tell even if you haven't told it.

When you have feedback from five other people (one of them an author of some standing), and you see some of them agreeing that something's not working, it takes an ego of Gibralter-sized proportions to think they're *all* wrong instead of considering that maybe/possibly something on the page isn't working the way you think. There's an appropriate line here from the movie, *The Battle of the Bulge:* "If ten men tell you your drunk, you better sit down."

After lunch there was a lecture from poet Harvey Hix. A lean, soft-spoken, prematurely gray gent, Hix's approach to examining the literary arts – as I'd find out over the course of the week – is consistently intellectual and analytical (Hix has also written books dealing with literary criticism and theory), and his lecture was a perfect example.

Hix focused on the book, *Philosophy in the Flesh,* by George Lakoff and Mark Johnson. Hix's examination got a bit esoteric for me, but it had something to do with the idea of the connection between certain categories of words and our physical reaction to those words and why we reacted to them. He brought in Kant and certain anthropological concepts, and a certain amount of this went over my head, but when he got to talking about how we responded to some words on a subconscious, almost primordial (or something like it) level, I began to kinda/sorta get what he was talking about. For instance, if I say "chair" to you, the idea of a chair is so deeply etched in your mental data bank, that there will be a physical response on your part to the word.

I went up to him afterward and talked with him a bit (everybody there, from staff lecturers to guests, was always open and approachable), and told him that somehow what he'd been saying reminded me of a 1950s sci fi flick, *Invaders from Mars*, which combined a juvenile flying saucer tale with haunting visuals and concepts that seemed to exercise the dynamic Hix was talking about. And while he was very open and supportive of the idea – "Yes! Exactly!" — a part of me was wondering – considering he'd brought up Kant and I was coming back with *Invaders from Mars* – if I didn't sound like some kind of moron.

There were more student readings, then dinner, then readings from the graduate students and one by my module mentor, Walter Cummins.

Cummins' essay concerned his time as a student under Philip Roth at a time when Roth was just breaking out as a literary star. It was a wonderfully warm yet fair portrait of an artist at an early point in his career, maybe a bit too full of himself (on one of Cummins' works, Roth had, early on, simply written in the margin, "Can't read any more"), but who could reel off ba-dum-*boom* rimshot one-liners so sharp and funny, Cummins remembered being in a neighboring classroom and still being able to hear the laughter from Roth's students.

That night – Sunday – was my first night in the dorm. The Fairleigh Dickinson online system fought me and I never got online throughout the week which was probably just as well. If I had, I probably would've spent my evenings on YouTube or other junk instead of things like, well, this, for instance.

This may have been a better dorm than the one I'd suffered through in my undergrad days, but a dorm bed is a dorm bed. They're built to last; not to provide comfort. Still, as my wife says, I could sleep on a sharp rock through a bomb blast.

MONDAY
The day opened with a pretty heavyweight lecture from one of the senior grad students, Cory Johnston. Mr. Johnston looked at three authors of Holocaust literature, all Holocaust survivors themselves – Primo Levi *(If This Is a Man)*, Aharon Appelfeld *(Badenheim 1939)*, and

Elie Weisel *(Night)*– to show how they effectively dealt with the most horrifying circumstances on the page through paradoxically simple, often emotionally detached prose, though each added their own, specific stylistic twist. Their deft understatement – a Hemingwayesque sort of minimalism — did more to convey the horror of the Holocaust than a torrent of emotional prose could have.

Then came Thomas E. Kennedy (most recent book: *Kerrigan in Copenhagen: A Love Story)*.

When I'd first learned of the FDU residency, I'd had visions of a bunch of arty literary types tossing literary esoterica back and forth in terms so arcane I probably would've thought I must've had a stroke because I'd know they were speaking English but still couldn't understand a word they were saying. And, yeah, I'd be lying if I didn't admit there is some of that both among the faculty and some of the students.

But Kennedy and his lecture – "How James Joyce Changed My Life as a Person and as a Writer" – was the flip side.

Critical aesthetic analysis, close reading, all of that heady academic stuff that can scare off the not-particularly-academic writer (like me), is (and I admit this reluctantly, but knowing the truth of it) a part of any serious development as a serious writer. You can't be good at this – I mean *really* good – without doing that due diligence.

But that's only half of it. What Tom Kennedy talked about was the other, equally necessary part: the passion — what it is the heart responds to on the page; what it is the heart wants to express on the page. That was what Kennedy brought to the party.

A mustachioed leprechaun of a guy in his 60s, Kennedy – disillusioned with the country's misadventure in Vietnam, feeling suffocated by the tangled web of family as well as their blind fealty to Catholicism – had moved to Copenhagen in the late '60s where he still lives for part of the year and makes his living as a writer (Kennedy has over 30 books to his credit ranging from novels to short stories and travel writing to studies of literature; Kennedy's honors include the O. Henry Award and the Pushcart Prize).

By his own admission, this wasn't to be an academic, analytic lecture; it was something personal, and so it was. He spoke about his father, a wannabe poet who submitted poems most of his life but only managed to get two into print. His father worked to instill his own love of books in his children. Kennedy told how, when he'd been a child, his father would read to him and his sibs every night telling them they were committed to hearing at least six pages, but could punch out after that. Every night, as his father got to the top of page seven, he'd ask: "Do you want me to go on?" And they did.

I have my own father issues, and they're connected to loss and writing as well, so maybe I was already predisposed to being exceptionally open to what Kennedy had to say. But we shared more than that.

Tom Kennedy's young life had been filled with books (he'd decided on being a writer after wading through Dostoyevsky's *Crime and Punishment*, pushed into his hands by his father), and he early on realized, "The authors of those books could be better friends to me than my friends..." Unlike the friends and family in his real life, these writers "...let me into their minds...(they) didn't hide things from me, or deceive me, and if they did, I could figure it out."

In this, what he had found in reading – and later in his writing – was much what I'd found as a book-loving youth; what I think most find who eventually venture into writing.

Kennedy developed a particular relationship with James Joyce whose work had a profound impact on his sense of himself as a person and as a writer. On reading Joyce's *Ulysses*, Kennedy said the novel provided him with "...an x-ray of human thought...(freed) me of the fear of looking into my own mind." "It is essential," Kennedy went on to say, "for a writer not to be afraid of his mind."

It was such an affecting talk that afterward I went up to him and tried to express what his piece had meant to me. I found myself having to cut myself short because in another few seconds I was going to start bawling. Sue me; I may not have an artist's talent, but I have an artist's soft, mushy heart.

Athletic, vivacious essayist/editor/reviewer Minna Proctor (we sometimes had 10-15 minutes between sessions; during one of those breaks, I saw her zoom off on her bicycle but back in time for the next session and not even breathing hard) followed with a practicum on book reviewing which, she pointed out, was not only a nice way for authors to pick up a few bucks, but involved an analytical process invaluable for studying how different authors do what they do (or fail to do what they're trying to do). It can – and should be — a form of aspiring author's homework.

What I found particularly interesting was how Ms. Proctor's "map" of the typical review closely echoed the concepts we freshman comp instructors try to get across to our students. I came out of the session figuring I didn't have any more chance of reviewing books than when I'd gone in, but I now had some new tools to bring to my comp classes in the fall.

After lunch, another graduate student lecture, this one from Kelly Jean Fitzsimmons; a hoot of a presentation on "The Brick Joke." "Brick joke" is the term for a joke that comes back around later in a routine, show, book, etc. and brings a laugh because of the familiarity of the piece.

Best example Ms. Fitzsimmons gave that most of you might know: the episode of *Seinfeld* where Kramer goes off to the beach to hit golf balls, then later, George – who's been lying to his prospective girlfriend about being a marine biologist – has to save a stranded whale suffocating from some obstruction in its blowhole which – you guessed it – turns out to be one of Kramer's golf balls.

It was a funny – yet wonderfully sharp – analysis of what is actually quite an elegantly designed device (when it works), and which, if nothing else, proved not all literary criticism has to necessarily be grim, drab, and boring. It certainly helped that Ms. Fitzsimmons' own gift for a laugh wasn't too shabby either.

And then before and after dinner, we were treated to literary critic James Wood who's *How Fiction Works* had been one of our assigned prep readings.

Frankly, I hadn't been nuts about the book. Maybe it was because Wood's examples were all from the literary cream which gave the book something of a snooty air. Maybe it was because he'd dumped on one of my personal favorites (John LeCarre). I got the sense of a literary snob, an effete intellectual elitist. Waiting for him to speak, I'd expected some guy in tweeds pooh-poohing anything people read for fun in a bored House of Lords English accent.

Instead, James Wood knocked me on my can. No tweeds, and while he did have a silky middle class English accent, what he also had was an enthusiasm, a wit, a quite unexpected (by me) warmth, and something his book didn't capture – a passion. What had seemed like intellectual calisthenics on the page I could now see was his heart responding to great writing with his intellect trying to figure out why.

In person, his arguments were also more nuanced. I overheard him talking with one of the other students, saying he'd *hated* the title of his book; that had been his publisher's idea (which makes sense marketing-wise; if you were a wannabe writer trying to learn to be a better writer, would you buy a book titled *How Fiction Works*, or one called, *One of the Myriad Ways Fiction Can Possibly Work on Occasion?*). When it came to writing, he didn't like that kind of definitiveness, and thought it was probably a flaw in his book; in *all* writing books. There was no *one* way to turn out good storytelling.

To make the point, he read excerpts from two books that he'd panned (generously not identifying the authors), but whose authors were well-respected and who'd turned out other books he'd liked. "I'm not reading them to pick on them," he said. "I just want you to see we've all been there."

He was also a splendid reader, with a fluid voice beautifully garlanded with that accent. Later, some of us joked – and I shared it with him – that, "If this literary criticism thing doesn't work out for you, we think you could do very well doing books-on-tape." He laughed saying it was probably because when he'd been a kid, he'd thought of becoming an actor.

But there was something else that came through in his readings besides providing a good show. It was clear – brilliantly, crystalline clear – in *how* he read the texts he used for his examples that he had a sharp, on-target understanding of the authors' intents. You could see why the guy had his job.

And he could write, too. After dinner, he read an essay he'd written about Keith Moon, the crazed, drug-saturated, antic-obsessed drummer for rock band The Who who'd died of an o.d. in 1978 at the age of 32. It was a beautifully written and frightfully smart piece; a smoothly blended mix of reflective nostalgia, analysis (damned if he couldn't write as well about classical and rock music as he did about lit), pop culture, and artistic principles which could be extended from the way rock's most manic drummer beat the skins to literary constructions.

At the end of the night I came away not having changed my mind about a lot of what he'd written in *How Fiction Works*, but believing that while one could disagree with James Wood (which I got the impression he wouldn't have a problem with), one could never dismiss him.

Between Tom Kennedy, Minna Proctor, and Mr. Wood, when my head hit the pillow that night, I thought *This* is what I was paying for.

By that time, I'd started getting a feel for the 30-40 students in the program. Each day – like a summer camp experience – you could see connections being made, strengthened, weave into networks. There was a wonderful, supportive sense of community that we all knew was spoiling us and would be hard to leave behind at the end of the residency. On more than one night, people who had been total strangers just a few days before ambled over in groups to a hotel abutting the campus to sit in the restaurant bar to chat over a nosh and a drink.

Ages ranged from fresh-out-of-undergrad to middle-aged (though I think only one other student was anywhere near my age among the incoming group). I'd ballpark it there was maybe a 60/40 split between the under-30 crowd and the overs.

They came from all over: Texas, D.C., Pennsylvania, Oregon, Wisconsin, Tennessee. One of the over-30s, Jeremy, had been living in Jersey for eight years but had never lost his syrupy-thick Kentucky accent (thankfully, I should say – it added great flavor to his wry stuff when he read).

The backgrounds were equally varied: ex-GI, advertising, bookkeeper for a construction company, public relations, corporate copywriter, ex-corrections officer, a couple of teachers from grade school to college, professional soccer ref. The youngsters were chasing a dream; the oldsters were often rebooting one.

The program offers paths through three genres – fiction, creative nonfiction, and poetry – and within each, styles and abilities seemed to range all over the dial. There was Anthony who wrote such off-the-wall stuff – like Lewis Carroll on acid – that I told him frankly, "It's so beyond my head I can't judge it, but I'm amazed by it." And then the young woman who courageously shared a new piece in an open reading, poignantly and almost poetically exploring her own feelings about her breakup just a few weeks before with the guy she'd been living with for four years. And then there was Jeremy's fiction piece, a comically understated piece of Southern heat about a battered wife who gets her revenge by shooting off her husband's nuts, then goes to the local whorehouse where he's spent way too much time and blows off the head of the local madam.

Like I said: varied.

The personalities ranged, too, from brash to self-effacing, bubbling to shy. Anthony liked to be around people, but didn't talk much. Chad seemed to be the group character (confirmed by his crazed reading of a wonderfully outrageous piece about a talking hamburger). Cornelius often seemed a bit reserved, reflective. One young woman, by her own admission, was a bit full of herself although – having landed a book contract with a small indie house even before she'd gotten to FDU – maybe not without reason. Some talked too much about themselves, some just liked to talk. We compared experiences, talked writing, talked writers, talked the difficulties of the writing life, and for some of us – most of us, I think, particularly the older students – it was the first time in a long time we could share that thinking with people who knew *exactly* what we were talking about because they were, more or less, in the same boat.

But many – even the older aspirants – had typically uninformed, unrealistic expectations about the hoped-for eventual payoff. The young lady with the book contract, for example, was wary about changing jobs because she wanted to keep herself available for book tours.

(When I was with Bantam, my first two books had rolled out with ads in places like *The New York Times*, *USA Today*, and *The Wall Street Journal*. My first novel got a starred review in *Publisher's Weekly*. And *I* didn't get any book tours or signings.

"We don't do signings," the Bantam PR guy assigned to my book had explained, "unless you're a big name. If you're not a name people already know, they won't come. Then you're sitting there, nobody's there, you're embarrassed, the store's embarrassed, we're embarrassed."

In a rather bruising confirmation of the Bantam guy's assertion, one of my aunts had managed to get me a book signing at a Barnes & Noble in south Jersey. In the two hours I sat there, only three people came up to my table, one only to see a "real author." Being the author, I don't know what the big deal was for him.)

Most of them would become disabused of those notions of glamorous book signings, interviews, of even making the barest living as a writer, on the following day.

TUESDAY

The previous night, when I'd made my regular call home to say hello and goodnight to my kids, I'd told my wife we were getting bused into New York City the next day.

"Aww, how cute! My honey's going on a school trip!"

Part of the FDU program is to give you some practical knowledge in how to get published and a realistic idea of the terrain. As kind of a prep, before the bus showed up, Minna Proctor led a practicum in writing cover letters for submitting material to literary magazines; the usual first stop for wannabe writers.

Proctor told us there were over 7300 lit magazines in the U.S. Getting published, she said, was about wading through them to find the right magazine for your work...and then hoping to God you caught the editor in the right mood when you submitted.

(I have to throw my two cents in here. The FDU crowd is always upbeat and optimistic; it's part of their job to get your confidence and energy up so you've got enough psychological stamina to take your run through the ball-busting, soul-sapping, confidence-killing gauntlet of trying to get published. And FDU isn't dealing with a bunch of the usual airy Creative Writing types; every member of the program was offered admission strictly on the basis of the material they'd submitted for review, so it was a given we were all people with respectable writing chops.

But once you cull away the lit magazines that look like somebody's high school book report, and the genre-specific mags, the flash fiction publications that only want page-long stuff…well, you'd be surprised how quickly that field starts to narrow.

And then there's the simple, blunt fact that there's always more people submitting than there's room for, 7300 magazines or no.)

Cover letters should be short, she said, opening with a quick few sentences on why you're submitting to that particular magazine, truthfully (I emphasize that) referencing the publication and some of their stories to show you've actually read it and know what they publish (we were warned about sucking up by lying about being a subscriber; "Some of them check"). If you've been referred to the magazine by someone whose name might bring you credibility in front of the editor, drop the name.

While you could take a chance and try, in your letter, to capture some of your wit and charm, not all editors appreciate that. As a general rule, assume you're not nearly as witty and charming as you think you are. Keep your letter clean and straightforward and professional, even if it's an online submission and you have to fill in those damned little boxes. Never just send something in with a flippant, "Enjoy!" or "Funsie!" as your cover letter. If this would be your first published work, say it; many lit editors get a buzz out of discovering new talent.

If you're rejected, don't get into a pissing match. Gracefully take the "no" and shut up. If you get something personalized, that makes suggestions, try to read between the lines to see if they're just being nice, or hinting they might reconsider the piece with those changes. Always be gracious, send thank you notes for their time, "Be ingratiating but not gross."

If you get a rejection that says, "This doesn't work for us but we'd like to see something else from you," resist the urge to start instantly shoveling stuff at them. Give it a few months, then reference their invite when you re-submit.

Rene Steinke mentioned some interesting stats on resubmission. The lit magazine *Tin House* had done some research in the wake of reports that a lot of the publishing industry – from who ran the show at the pub houses, what books got published, etc. to which books are reviewed in major venues like *The New York Times Literary Review* – tilt heavily male. *Tin House* did some research of their own, and found that, for whatever reason, when offered the chance to resubmit, 88% of men will resubmit, but only 13% of women writers will.

So, for you women writers out there, in just this regard you need to be as pigheaded and narcissistic and rapaciously ambitious as men.

Understand what a given publication prints and what they *don't* print. Don't send lit pieces to a mag running Goth horror flash fiction. Not only will you get a quick rejection, but you'll tick them off, maybe burn a bridge, and get yourself labeled as an idiot. Pay attention to submission guidelines and don't think your stuff is so damned good the editor will waive them just for you.

Tom Kennedy told a hoot of a resubmission story. He'd gotten five rejections in a row from *The Sewanee Review* at which point the editor sent a rather snotty crotch-kick of a letter to Kennedy saying he should stop sending them stories and find "a more minor forum" more appropriate for his material.

Understandably, that got Kennedy's fire up. He turned to his wife saying, "I *have* to answer this guy! What should I send?"

What he sent was another story…which they published along with his next few.

Then we climbed on the bus, forty-odd minutes later we were in Greenwich Village, parked on Christopher Street in front of the building housing The Council of Literary Magazines and Presses, an advisory group for the lit print crowd. We sat for an hour with the director of the CLMP, Jeffrey Lependorf, as he walked us through the world of big and small house publishing, but most critically for those who've never been published before, the ever-expanding galaxy of lit magazines, both in print and online.

In terms of submitting, he confirmed much of what Minna Proctor had told us that morning. He also advised in answer to the perennial question, "What should I be writing?" not to worry about it. Write what interests you; write it as best you can. "Because if you try to write what's popular now, by the time you're done they'll be on to the next thing."

As upbeat as he tried to be, some frank numbers let a bit of air out of a few sails in the room. Yes, there are breakout hits, phenoms, it happens (my suitemate Jeff told me about a fellow student in a class he'd taken under Rene Steinke in New York who'd manage to cop himself a deal with HarperCollins with a 100,000 copy first run of his first novel). *But...*

The *typical* run for an author's first book is between 5-7,000 copies with a probable advance of $35,000 (my experience: between taxes and your agent's commission – and if you landed a book at a major house, you did it through an agent – you walk out with fifty cents on the dollar). And that's from a major house. At small indie houses, you're looking at runs of 1500-2500, and small advances…if any (at this news, a lot of quiet "Ewww"'s from some students).

On the other hand, a small house is more likely to get behind a book (although it has fewer resources to get behind a book with). For those who might've been thinking, How the hell am I supposed to get people to buy my books without some marketing, Lependorf had this to say: "Marketing doesn't create the business; marketing *follows* the business." In other words, the money either goes behind proven names, or marketing muscle gets committed *after* a book demonstrates traction in the marketplace.

The news was worse for poets. To put it bluntly, if you're a poet, you're pretty much screwed. Lependorf put it more nicely: "Yours will be a world of literary magazines and small presses." Unless you're Maya Angelou, big houses can't make money on poetry, and a small house press run for a poetry book typically runs 500-700 copies.

What's worth noting about some of those stats is how they match up against what I experienced when I worked in publishing at what was then Elsevier-Dutton (which went back to its original name of E.P. Dutton after Elsevier shed us, then got glommed up by Penguin in 1986 which, in turn, was glommed up by Random House right about the time of our visit) back in the early 1980s. The number for first novel print runs hasn't changed which is interesting – and a bit depressing – because there's about 50 million more people living in the U.S. now.

And, adjusted for inflation, first-time advances don't seem to have improved much either.

In other words, life sucks for the first-time author; it always did, and it undoubtedly always will.

(My undergrad writing professor, novelist/short story writer/essayist/screenwriter William Price Fox, told us on our first day, "Don't write for money or to be famous. Most of you won't make any money, and most of you won't become famous. You do this because you *want* to.")

Someone asked about self-publishing using some online tools. Lependorf advised against it. Again, not that there weren't success stories, but getting the book printed is the smallest hurdle.

"We have a joke," he said. "A book is printed…not *published* until it's in a reader's hands." One usually finds in the self-published community that the success stories involve authors who spend 27 hours a day day-in-day-out shilling, promoting, networking, and that they represent a staggeringly small percentage of self-published authors.

We were on our own for a few hours until we all hooked up again at the New York Public Library for a lecture on and a look at the Berg Collection; items like original Mark Twain manuscripts, and Charles Dickens' marked-up reading copies of "A Christmas Carol" from his reading tour of America in 1860s. For the true appreciator of literature it was a buzz to see those kinds of things up close. Twain has always been one of my favorites, and getting a look at the hand-written manuscript for *A Connecticut Yankee in King Arthur's Court* – to be a nose-length away from a piece of literary history — was very affecting.

As interesting were some of the curator's stories. The library had materials which allowed you to see how authors had developed certain books. The germ of an idea for one of Virgina Woolf's novels can be seen popping up in some correspondence, then a bit more developed in a few notes jotted some time later, and then, of course, through various drafts of her manuscripts.

It was a nice way of finding out nobody – even the greats – get it right the first time…or even all at once. The curator told us that while Jack Kerouac affected being a free spirited, jazz-styled writer riffing on the page, bragging he'd written *On the Road* in just three weeks, "He may have *typed* it in three weeks, but he was working on it for *four years!*" Some of that work included a page of over 100 possible titles before his editor pushed for *On the Road*.

WEDNESDAY

Half-way through the residency, the long days were getting to me. Or maybe it was the trip to New York. During that hole in the day between the CLMP and the New York Public Library, I'd covered – by my count – about 80 blocks, killing time by drifting past familiar locales from my days working in the city, but mostly trying to find a clean bathroom accessible to the public. My knees are shot anyway, so when I woke up Wednesday morning, ol' Trigger was feeling it wouldn't be a bad idea for Roy to take me behind the barn, put me down and sell me for dog food. I was feeling like dog food looks anyway.

I wasn't the only one feeling the drag of long days day after day. As I walked across campus with Jeremy, he called the experience "A writer's boot camp," and neither one of us could, at that point, even remember what day it was.

I was also getting itchier. The dorm windows don't have screens. At night, I'd find myself batting at the shadows flitting through the light from my small desk lamp, the brightest light in the room (as comfortable as the dorms – for dorms – were, one of their deficiencies, along with not having screens on the windows, were they were quite dim. Each bedroom has one dull light sconce, and other than the light in the kitchen and bathroom, there are no overhead lights in the suites). And the mosquitoes seemed to be working their way in from the extremities. By Wednesday morning, I had a mosquito bite on each wrist, one on my right foot, another on my left ankle.

That morning, Walter Cummins conducted a workshop "On Writing the Essay on Craft." One of the requirements for the FDU degree is a 5-10 page essay in which, by focusing on a single book, the work of a single author, or some other clearly defined target, the writer explores an element of craft (Cory Johnston's and Kelly Jean Fitzsimmons' presentations came from their craft essays). While this sounds like the typical college term paper – and at one point at FDU, that's what the craft essay was – the program has tweaked the model, wanting something more personal, crossing the analytical aspects of an academic paper but presented within a more creative, less neutral framework.

(To support the writing of the essay, which comes late in the program, MFA students craft two "close readings" during each module: 1-2 page papers examining an aspect of craft in a particular book. They're also expected to read 50 books over the course of the two-year program.)

After lunch, groups of students met with the mentors of their fall second modules. Jeff Allen – a prize-winning author of long and short fiction as well as an essayist and reviewer — was my second module mentor. Allen – a more low-key personality than the bubbling Walter Cummins – demonstrated one of the many strengths of the program: that over the course of one's two years there, the student will deal with an almost dizzying variety of mentors, each with a different sensibility, different perspective, different approach, but all sharing the goal of guiding students toward better writing. That range of perspectives, combined with peer feedback, provides a view outside one's head most non-professional writers have little opportunity to acquire.

That evening, Minna Proctor interviewed Sam Lipsyte who later read from his most recent short story collection, *The Fun Parts.*

The Fun Parts was a return to his origins for Lipsyte. His first book had been a collection of short stories, many of which had already been published in magazines, and then he'd followed that with a novel "Because that's what you do, right? Your first book is short stories, then you do a novel." Two more novels had followed, and then Lipsyte thought it would be interesting to, as a more developed and experienced writer, go back to the form with which he'd started.

I'd had a problem with Lipsyte's work. He's undeniably a strong writer with impeccable craftsmanship and a blazing imagination, but – in my eyes – his stories were laced with a misanthropy and an almost Artaudian calculation to shock and disturb I couldn't connect with. Based on his work, I'd expected Lipsyte to be some acidic, abrasive smartass – kind of a literary Tucker Max.

Sam Lipsyte was my second, humbling lesson – after James Wood – in not confusing the man with the work. He actually seemed very gentle, straightforward, comfortable in sharing his experiences without once coming off with a "I'm the Big Dog in the room" attitude (I should probably know better after Mr. Wood and Mr. Lipsyte, but I'll still wager we wouldn't have gotten that vibe from Tucker Max), quite smart and understanding of his own process (not as common as you think; it takes most beginning writers some time to get a handle on how their own head works and how best to get the most, best work out of it). I can't say I like his work much more than I did before, but, as with Wood, I developed a much greater respect for the man as a writer.

(At this point it's probably also worth mentioning that just because you like something doesn't make it good, or that disliking something makes it bad. Just because you like McD's doesn't make it Kobe beef. One of the intellectual tools requiring development in a serious writer – and the FDU requirement of 12 close readings over the course of the program is intended to cultivate this – is being analytical enough to differentiate between one's own subjective tastes, and the caliber of craftsmanship in a piece of work.

I call it the Twinkie/Broccoli Paradigm. Given a choice between a Twinkie and a piece of broccoli, most people will opt for the Twinkie. This doesn't make Twinkies good for you.)

One of the questions students asked Lipsyte during his Q & A – and which was one of the two questions regularly asked by students when they got in close proximity to an author along with, "How'd you sell your first book?" – was about his process. When asked if he outlined, Lipsyte said not for his short stories, but for his novels, yet even then it was just a few notes. "I find that if I do a (detailed) outline, I look at it after and go, 'I'm done.'"

One insight he shared I was particularly struck by was in answer to an observation that some stories in the collection contained a lot of action, while others had very little. "Sometimes," said Lipsyte, "the language of the story *is* the story."

THURSDAY

By now, a lot of us were dragging, although in some cases it had a lot to do with the nightly late hours over at the hotel restaurant bar. I still had one bug bite on each wrist, but the ones around my ankles were multiplying. It was only a matter of time before the blood-sucking armies of the night began making deep probes into the interior lands.

In the morning, Walter Cummins' module had its second meeting, group members having had time to reflect on the feedback from our Sunday session, and to have some one-on-one time with Walter to discuss thoughts and plans on going forward.

As Cummins and I talked about my own plans for going forward with my chosen piece, we discussed his own process. An impressive fiction writer and essayist, Cummins "couldn't do novels." There was something about the long form he couldn't bang through, while he was perfectly comfortable with shorter forms.

With each Q & A with visiting talent, with each exchange with a member of the faculty, one of the lessons students can't help but absorb – reinforcing what James Wood had said – that there's no one way to write, no one process, that no two writers are alike. They are, after all, human beings (one likes to think), and in the same way that even people with much in common still have their differences, each writer's mind is unique and distinct unto itself. They have different affinities, different strengths, different comfort zones.

Now, while that may be a bit confusing and daunting for the beginner – "So what do *I* do?" – what it means is *Try them;* try them all, all the processes, all the systems, and in that testing, you'll undoubtedly find what works best for you.

My one-on-one was followed by the indestructible Ellen Akins leading a workshop in Point of View where she walked us through the various perspectives from which a story could be told. A direct but sharply insightful woman, Akins – along with being a novelist, and writer of short stories, articles and reviews – is also the recipient of The Literature Award of the American Academy of Arts and Letters. That's my way of saying when Ellen Akins had something to say – about your work, about writing in general – you'd be a fool not to listen.

From Akins, I'd already gotten some of the most valuable advice I think I've ever received concerning writing. I'd heard something akin to it from a grad assistant when I'd been an undergrad at the University of South Carolina, but it was nice to hear the idea recharged by a mind as impressive as hers.

It had been Akins' group which had been rolled into Cummins', so now back on campus, she'd sat in with us for our second get-together. We were talking about one particular piece and the conversation had drifted into the area of should/shouldn'ts could/couldn'ts. "You can do *anything*," she'd said, "as long as you do it beautifully." And then, like a verbal parenthetical, she added, "You might also be asking for trouble."

After lunch we gathered for a panel of several alumni who gave us some idea of the possibilities and frustrations which might follow graduation. They'd all graduated between 2004 (FDU's first graduating MFA class) and 2008, I think. Jena Salon had since gone on to become editor of *TLR,* the school's literary magazine (don't get the idea this is one of those little mags a school does for its students; *TLR* is an internationally-respected literary magazine. In fact, FDU students cannot submit work until after graduation to prevent conflict of interest). Kevin Carey, an older gentleman, was a writing teacher while still banging away at getting his poetry published (he'd gotten a few into ink).

One young woman now writing under the name Lisa Van Allen (she had taken a new pen name to launch a "new brand" in the market to differentiate her recent work from her old) seemed, in just the four-five years since her graduation, on track to a successful career as a novelist, having published several books and doing well enough to quit her day job.

She held a frankly pragmatic perspective. She'd found a profitable niche writing commercial fiction for the female audience (I was a little uncomfortable in that she sounded a bit apologetic about "commercial" writing). She still wrote for lit magazines, with her commercial stuff essentially buying her the latitude to indulge in work that had a more personal value.

During the Q & A session, one of the young students asked about the value of drumming up an audience through Facebook, Twitter, etc.

– the various online platforms.

She said she didn't think it mattered. A premise with enough of a twist to get people talking – "The kind of thing that *makes* you want to talk about it with other people" – was the real igniter. She had asked the publicist at her pub house this very same thing. As far as the publicist could tell, use of social media didn't seem to have any predictable effect on moving books or not moving books. "I guess," the publicist told her, "we don't really know what sells books."

As far as her own process, she "started with a premise" because that's what her publishers bought. In the arena of pitching movies, I supposed you'd call it the hook. It's that short thing of a couple of lines that seems to capture the general thrust of a work and which makes editors and producers and network programming execs go, "I get it!"

The remainder of the day was dedicated to alumni as well. There followed a screening of *All That Lies Between Us,* a documentary self-produced and directed by FDU alums Kevin Carey and Mark Hilringhouse (and scored by another grad, Bob Evans) profiling Maria Gillan, something of a patron saint of New Jersey poets.

Afterward, there was a reception featuring a number of visiting alumni, capped off with readings from several graduate students, faculty member Renee Ashley reciting from her latest poetry collection *(Because I am the Shore I Want to Be The Sea),* and capped off with Tom Kennedy reading from his most recently released novel, *Kerrigan in Copenhagen.*

FRIDAY

I came back from my morning stroll (a habit I'd gotten into early on; the rolling terrain of the FDU campus might've been hard on my knees, but it made for a lovely walk/jog/run depending on your leanings) and found that, having little fresh meat to attack on my ankles, I now had mosquito bites on my upper right calf. Could I make it to Sunday before being completely devoured?

My suitemate and I had been brooding all morning over the upcoming workshop: "Logic for Poets." Neither of us were much for poetry. Actually, that's a bit of an understatement. Neither of us *understood* poetry. At all.

It's a lesson in how we can find ourselves imprisoned by our sensibilities. I'd grown up in a household of voracious readers, but my mom and dad read mainstream commercial fiction, mostly mysteries. That's what was in the house, so that's what I grew up reading. I took up with Alistair MacLean when other kids were reading The Hardy Boys. By the time I was exposed to more literary forms – in high school and then in college – I found it extremely difficult (partly because I was so damned intellectually lazy and nearsighted) to cultivate a taste for more challenging fare (Tom Kennedy's dad knew what he was doing handing him *Crime and Punishment* when he was a kid; prime the pump early, parents!).

Over the years, I've tried to compensate by making a conscious effort to self-educate myself, reading some of the literary greats from Homer (I could do *The Odyssey; The Iliad,* not so much) to Dickens (Wow!) to Pynchon (I gave up). I found that as long as the work had a recognizable narrative form, there was something I could usually mentally grab hold of. But for me, trying to get a handle on poetry was like watching a cat try to climb a glass window; no purchase.

In that regard, for me, Renee Ashley's workshop "Logic for Poets" was like a star shell going off in the night: blinding.

I already knew some of the basics; poetry doesn't follow the "rules" of prose. It may use the tools of narrative, character, dialogue, etc., but it will use them as the poet pleases. Poetry doesn't break the rules of prose; it lives *outside* them in a non-linear, abstract world.

Prose, Ashley explained, is a closed logic system. "It's like the manual for operating your refrigerator," she said. "If you leave a step out, your yogurt goes bad."

Poetry, in contrast, is an "open" system, which has more in common with music and free-running imagination than narrative forms.

She displayed two photographs of walls of field stone: one "dry," built by deftly fitting the stones together, and the other "wet," with the stones held together by cement. Poetry was a dry stone wall, interlaced with gaps; poems don't tell you everything, they don't explain. Prose is a wet wall; all the gaps are filled; there is no flexibility, no give, no breathing room for the grand, gorgeous leaps the mind takes in the spaces between the stones in poetry's dry wall.

Poetry, Ashley explained, is "associative" – the usual logical connecting steps typical of prose (the cement in the wall) aren't there. A given poem may have many different logics operating sequentially, simultaneously, occasionally. Sometimes the speed of association is the heart of a poem rather than the meaning of its words.

Another analogy: "Prose goes in the front door, says what it has to say, and leaves. Poetry goes through the back door, the window, the vents, *anywhere* but the front door."

As Ashley presented us with one analogy after another, the nature of poetry became even more clear in that the only way to describe its nature, its joys, its gossamer structure was through analogy. Poetry is often about describing the indescribable; creating a sensation which may have little or nothing to do with the literal meanings of words. Why should talking *about* it be any different?

(Although Renee Ashley and Harvey Hix seemed like night and day to me in how they talked about poetry – Ashley with a passion so hot I sometimes thought she was going to burst into flame, and Hix with a coolly analytical precision — I could see the overlap between Ashley's talk of "association" and Hix's lecture of several days earlier offering the idea of near-instinctive physical responses to certain categories of words; both went beyond the step-by-step nature of prose.)

For the first time, I had some kind of understanding of how poetry works. As I told Ashley afterward, "I may still never know a good poem if it poked me in the eye, and I sure as hell won't ever be able to write a good one (she described my effort in the workshop as "good bad Beckett"), but now I know why they work the way they do." What I also caught from her – even though I might not share it – is why poets and poetry lovers have a love for the form.

But Renee Ashley offered us another lesson that day; one that caught the true, encompassing philosophy of the FDU program. "We don't teach you how to write," she said. "We teach you how to think differently than you did before…It's called 'brain mobility'…You have to travel some roads you don't know. You have to learn to play again… You have to learn to read as a writer."

Another essential difference between prose and poetry: "If you write prose, you're gonna get paid." Poets don't make money, but with that comes a "…freedom to express yourself to your ultimate ability."

That afternoon we were treated to a Q & A between Rene Steinke and author Lydia Millet who later, after dinner, read from her most recent novel, *Magnificence*.

Again, here was a work I didn't connect with, but it was simply a matter of taste (I doubt Ms. Millet would like my WW II tales). Still, it was obvious to me in reading *Magnificence* why the lady had been a finalist for the Pulitzer (for her third novel, *My Happy Life)* with writing that manages to be both elegant yet clean, and always smart. She was just as smart – and witty – in discussing her own process and development as a writer.

Millet had begun getting serious in writing in college about the time she'd stopped being serious about singing opera. "The idea of recitals in front of a lot of people made me want to throw up."

Unlike Lisa Van Allen who begins with a premise, Lydia Millet starts "…with an idea of a feeling, and I write to that feeling…I want (the book) to have a certain sense, a tonal quality I want to end on."

She doesn't calculate. In *Magnificence,* she didn't work from plot point A to B to C, but wrote instinctively.

I think she also went a healthy distance in deromanticizing the picture of the writer's life many of the students had. She still holds a day job (as a copyeditor), has a family, and finds herself often writing in breaks squeezed into her day, sometimes as short as 15-30 minutes. It's obviously hard to get a handle on what you're writing in those kinds of fits and starts, but the trick is not to second-guess yourself while you're still trying to plow through a draft. "The longer you can suspend the critical part of yourself until you finish, great. Then put it away and come back to it and *then* be harsh."

She's not happy with her early works. Her first novel – *Omnivores* – was published when she was just 26 (she'd written it when she was 24), and looking back at it now she feels it was written in too much of a hurry. It was also marked – as were several of her early books – by a cocky, young cynicism she now regrets, and even admitted to being embarrassed by. "As I grew older, I wrote more emotionally, I pulled back from a young cynicism…" one takes on "…because it's cool."

"If you go back to a book you wrote ten years ago and think it's perfect," Lydia Millet said, "I think you're mentally ill."

SATURDAY

By Saturday, quite a few of us were, well, there's no polite way of putting this: dragging ass. No doubt that had been taken into account in the plotting of the residency, and Saturday was a fairly light day.

There was a morning workshop conducted by Minna Proctor on MFA students reading for FDU's literary magazine, *TLR*.

Established in 1957 – making it one of the older literary magazines in the country — *TLR* is a quarterly publishing about 1000 pages of fiction, poetry, essays and reviews per year. As I said earlier, this isn't a college lit magazine, but a literary publication accepting submissions from all over the world to put together collections of the best work available to them.

Proctor was frank about the subjectivity of the reading process not just at *TLR*, but any lit magazine or publisher. She offered a cautionary tale concerning *The New Yorker*, a magazine widely viewed as the top of the heap when it comes to publishing short fiction. In an experiment that has been regularly repeated every ten years or so, someone took an old *The New Yorker* short story and sent it around to other lit magazines only to have it rejected. At times, it's even been rejected by *The New Yorker*.

This much I'd already learned from my own experiences both in publishing and in screenwriting; that sometimes landing a sale came down to getting a piece of work in front of the right set of eyes at just the right time when the owner of those eyes is in just the right mood.

That evening was a graduation dinner for MFA grads. It was a simple, rather informal, but touching ceremony. A mentor would make a short speech about one of his or her charges – one that was as much about the character of the writer as it was about their work – then the graduate would make a speech, and finally be formally granted their degree by the dean.

Writing isn't like being an accountant or a business major. The rewards are so iffy, the drive to create so illogical and passionate, it takes a toll not only on the writer, but to the friends and family around the writer as well. Every grad acknowledged, in often tearful terms, the support and love and forbearance of those close to them. It got to the point where I had to leave the room; I was getting misty over people I didn't even know!

I wasn't the only one. I think it was a combination of the nature of the evening, and the fact that it was our last night together, and also that there was an open bar, that some of us gathered out on the veranda of The Mansion in a bit of a reflective, sentimental mood.

We were a small group, working together intensely every day. Some of us had forged particularly strong connections and shared stories not just about writing but about families, spouses, lives. Some of us would see each other in Wroxton in a few months; for others – like myself – it would be a year.

Which probably explains what happened to me the next day.

SUNDAY

The only scheduled event is a light breakfast and the remainder of student readings. I was in that bunch.

I'd picked a piece I'd written last year for Sound on Sight, a movie and TV site I'd been contributing to for several years. The piece was about my mother who'd died early that year.

I'd chosen it for practical reasons: it could be easily cut down to our allowed reading time of five minutes, and it could stand alone (a number of students had read from excerpts from longer works, like novels they were working on, but I felt they didn't stand that well on their own). After that general maudlin feeling the previous night of, "I love you, man!" I now started worrying that maybe the emotion of the piece might get to me.

That morning, before breakfast, I walked around the campus running the piece over and over in my head, and even finding myself a nice sunny rock to sit on and read it out loud hoping that the repetition would beat some of the sentiment out of it.

I almost made it through the reading. Folded up with two lines to go.

I'm still trying to figure out how to do what I need to do over the next two years while holding down my various adjunct gigs. And writing at home when the grass needs cutting, the dog needs walking, the kids need to be ferried here and there is a lot harder than sitting alone in a quiet dorm room, revved up from a day of writers and writing, yet with a focus the silent hours of the night also gave me.

But however well or poorly I do from this point on, they were 10 great days, the kind of days aspiring, struggling, misunderstood, and often lonely writers hope for.

CONTRIBUTORS

CHARLES ARDAI is an American entrepreneur, writer, editor, and television producer. He is best known as founder and CEO of Juno, an Internet company, and founder and editor of Hard Case Crime, a line of pulp-style paperback crime novels.

Ardai's writing has appeared in mystery magazines such as *Ellery Queen's Mystery Magazine* and *Alfred Hitchcock's Mystery Magazine*, gaming magazines such as *Computer Gaming World* and *Electronic Games*, and anthologies such as *Best Mysteries of the Year* and *The Year's Best Horror Stories*. Ardai has also edited numerous short story collections such as *The Return of the Black Widowers*, *Great Tales of Madness and the Macabre*, and *Futurecrime*. His first novel, *Little Girl Lost*, was published in 2004 and was nominated for both the Edgar Allan Poe Award by the Mystery Writers of America, and the Shamus Award by the Private Eye Writers of America; his second, *Songs of Innocence*, was called "an instant classic" by the *Washington Post*, selected as one of the best books of the year by *Publishers Weekly*, and won the Shamus Award. Both books were written under the alias Richard Aleas and have been optioned for the movies by Universal Pictures. Ardai previously received a Shamus nomination for the short story "Nobody Wins," and he received the Edgar Award in 2007 for the short story "The Home Front". In 2015, he received the Ellery Queen Award for his work on Hard Case Crime.

Ardai's third novel, *Fifty-to-One*, was published in November 2008. It was the fiftieth book in the Hard Case Crime series and the first to be published under Ardai's real name.

His fourth novel, *Hunt Through the Cradle of Fear*, is part of a pulp adventure series he created in 2009, describing the globetrotting exploits of a modern-day explorer named Gabriel Hunt. Authorship of all the books in this series is credited to Gabriel Hunt himself.

In 2010, he began working as a writer and producer on the SyFy television series *Haven*, inspired by the Hard Case Crime novel, *The Colorado Kid*, by Stephen King. The first episode of *Haven* aired on July 9, 2010.

In addition to his writing and publishing activities, Ardai serves as a managing director of the D. E. Shaw group.

Ardai attended Columbia University, where he graduated *summa cum laude* in 1991.

MAX ALLAN COLLINS was hailed in 2004 by *Publisher's Weekly* as "a new breed of writer." A frequent Mystery Writers of America "Edgar" nominee in both fiction and non-fiction categories, he has earned an unprecedented eighteen Private Eye Writers of America "Shamus" nominations, winning for his Nathan Heller novels, *True Detective* (1983) and *Stolen Away* (1991), receiving the PWA life achievement award, the Eye, in 2007.

His graphic novel *Road to Perdition* (1998) is the basis of the Academy Award-winning 2002 film starring Tom Hanks, Paul Newman, and Daniel Craig, directed by Sam Mendes. It was followed by two acclaimed prose sequels, *Road to Purgatory* (2004) and *Road to Paradise* (2005), and a graphic novel sequel, *Return to Perdition* (2011). He has written a number of innovative suspense series, including Nolan (the author's first series, about a professional thief), Quarry (the first series about a hired killer), and Eliot Ness (four novels about the famous real-life Untouchable's Cleveland years). He is completing a number of "Mike Hammer" novels begun by the late Mickey Spillane, with whom Collins did many projects.

His many comics credits include the syndicated strip *Dick Tracy* (1977 — 1993); his own *Ms. Tree* (longest-running private eye comic book); *Batman*; and *CSI: Crime Scene Investigation*, based on the hit TV series for which he has also written video games, jigsaw puzzles, and ten novels that have sold millions of copies worldwide.

He has been termed "the novelization king" by *Entertainment Weekly*, with tie-in books on the *USA Today* bestseller list nine times and the *New York Times* list three times. His movie novels include *Saving Private Ryan*, *Air Force One*, and *American Gangster*, which won the Best

Novel "Scribe" Award in 2008 from the International Association of Tie-in Writers.

An independent filmmaker in the Midwest, he has written and directed five features and two documentaries, including the Lifetime movie *Mommy* (1996) and a 1997 sequel, *Mommy's Day*. He wrote *The Expert*, a 1995 HBO World Premiere, and *The Last Lullaby*, starring Tom Sizemore, a 2008 feature film based on Collins' acclaimed novel, *The Last Quarry*; the film won numerous awards on the film festival circuit before its theatrical and home-video release.

His one-man show, *Eliot Ness: An Untouchable Life*, was nominated for an Edgar for Best Play of 2004 by the Mystery Writers of America; a film version, written and directed by Collins, was released on DVD in 2008 and appeared on PBS stations in 2009. His documentary, *Caveman: V.T. Hamlin & Alley Oop*, was also released on DVD after screening on PBS stations. A new edit of his 1999 documentary, *Mike Hammer's Mickey Spillane*, is featured on the Criterion Collection's DVD and Blu-ray of the classic film noir, *Kiss Me Deadly*.

His other credits include film criticism, short fiction, songwriting, trading-card sets, and a regular column in *Asian Cult Cinema* magazine. His non-fiction work has received many honors, with his coffee-table book *The History of Mystery* receiving nominations for every major mystery award, and his recent *Men's Adventure Magazines* (with George Hagenauer) winning the Anthony Award. With Jim Traylor, he received an Edgar nomination for *Mickey Spillane's Mike Hammer: One Lonely Knight* (1984); recently the two authors teamed for *Mickey Spillane on Screen* (2012).

BENJAMIN B. DUNLAP is a teacher, scholar, author, performing artist, writer/producer for Public Television, and former college president who, in addition to speaking engagements around the world, has designed and moderated conferences and seminars in this country and abroad for the Aspen Institute and other organizations since 1985. Winner of numerous awards for teaching and scholarship, his faculty appointments over a span of 51 years have been at Harvard University as an instructor, assistant professor, and visiting professor; The University of South Carolina as a Carolina Professor; and Wofford College as the Chapman Family Professor in the Humanities. In addition to his 13 years as President of Wofford College, he was twice appointed a Fulbright Senior Lecturer in Thailand and was an inaugural Japan Society Leadership Fellow in Tokyo.

As an award-winning writer-producer for Public Television from 1974 through the early '90's, he is credited with major responsibility for more than a hundred programs and series including dramas, documentaries, performing arts, and distance learning projects. Listed as one of "Fifty Remarkable People" for the international 2007 TED conference in Monterey, Dunlap's presentation has been viewed via the internet by well over a million people.

Named President *Emeritus* of Wofford College in 2013, Dunlap holds a B.A. degree, *summa cum laude*, from Sewanee: The University of the South, where he was a George F. Baker Scholar; B.A. and M.A. degrees from Oxford University, where he was a Rhodes Scholar; and a Ph.D. from Harvard University, where he was a James A. Rumrill Scholar. He has received honorary degrees from Sewanee, Wofford, and the University of South Carolina as well as the South Carolina Governor's Award in the Humanities and the Order of the Palmetto, South Carolina's highest civilian award. For four years he was a soloist and principal dancer with the Columbia City Ballet, and his publications include essays, fiction, poetry, and an opera libretto.

SONNY GROSSO remains one of the most decorated policemen in the New York City Police Department's history, spending 22 memorable years in the Police Department. In his last ten years on the force, he was segueing into the entertainment business after he and his partner Eddie Egan's bust of "The French Connection" case was turned into a best-selling book, and, in 1971, an eight-time nominated and five-time Academy Award-winning movie. *The French Connection* was named one of the "AFI's 100 Greatest American Movies," and was also selected to the "National Film Registry, Library of Congress" in 2005. Recently, "The National Law Enforcement Officers Museum" honored Sonny Grosso with a special premiere showing of *The French Connection* at their first annual Film Festival.

He has co-written and/or contributed to four books including *Point Blank*, and he has won several entertainment honors including Gemini, *TV Guide*, and National Academy Television Arts & Sciences Awards. Personally, he has received numerous honors, including, the "1997 Ellis Island Medal of Honor" (awarded to people who have made a major contribution to society), the "Detectives Endowment Association Man of the Year," "The Colombia Association Man of the Year," and the "Leadership in Cinema and Entertainment" (from the Coalition of Italo-American Associations).

Grosso has spent 35 plus years in the entertainment business initially becoming a renowned technical advisor on several legendary movies including *The Godfather* and *The Seven-Ups*, and also on several classic TV series including *Kojak* and *Baretta*. In 1980, he joined forces with Larry Jacobson to form a highly successful production company, Grosso Jacobson Entertainment, which has produced about 800 hours of television movies and series, primarily in the crime and law enforcement genre, including ten Mary Higgins Clark movies, and the top-rated and critically acclaimed CBS series, *Top Cops*.

RICHARD HERMAN served in the U.S. Air Force for 21 years, retiring in 1983 with the rank of major. Since then, he has authored 14 novels including *The Warbirds* (1988), *Against All Enemies* (1998), and *Edge of Honor* (1999).

During his years in the Air Force, Herman flew C-130s as a navigator, and F-4s as a weapons system officer. He logged over 240 combat missions during two tours in Southeast Asia. He also taught at the Air Force Academy and served as an operations plans officer.

KIER-LA JANISSE is a film writer and programmer, the founder of The Miskatonic Institute of Horror Studies and Owner/Editor-in-Chief of *Spectacular Optical*. She has been a programmer for the Alamo Drafthouse Cinema and Fantastic Fest in Austin, Texas, co-founded Montreal microcinema Blue Sunshine, founded the CineMuerte Horror Film Festival in Vancouver (1999-2005,) and was the subject of the documentary *Celluloid Horror* (2005).

She has written for *Filmmaker, Shindig!, Incite: Journal of Experimental Media, Rue Morgue* and *Fangoria* magazines, has contributed to *The Scarecrow Movie Guide* (Sasquatch Books, 2004) and *Destroy All Movies!! The Complete Guide to Punks on Film* (Fantagraphics, 2011), and is the author of *A Violent Professional: The Films of Luciano Rossi* (FAB Press, 2007) and *House of Psychotic Women: An Autobiographical Topography of Female Neurosis in Horror and Exploitation Films* (FAB Press, 2012). She co-edited *KID POWER!* and *Satanic Panic: Pop-Cultural Paranoia in the 1980s* with Paul Corupe, and is currently writing *A Song From the Heart Beats the Devil Every Time*, about children's programming from 1965-1985.

THOMAS E. KENNEDY's 30-plus books include novels, story and essay collections, literary criticism, translation, and anthologies, most recently the four stand-alone novels of the *Copenhagen Quartet*, all from Bloomsbury worldwide, each set in a different season in Copenhagen and written in a different style – *In the Company of Angels* (2010), *Falling Sideways* (2011), *Kerrigan in Copenhagen* (2013), and *Beneath the Neon Egg* (2014) — as well as his *Getting Lucky: New & Selected Stories, 1982-2012* (New American Press, 2013).

Hundreds of Kennedy's stories and essays appear regularly in such magazines as *Esquire, The Independent, The New Yorker on-line, Epoch, The Southern Review, New Letters*, and many others, and have won the O. Henry Prize, two Pushcart Prizes, a National Magazine Award, a Charles Angoff Award, two Eric Hoffer Awards, and many other distinctions. His translations have appeared in *American Poetry Review, Epoch, Ecotone, New Letters, The Literary Review, Poet Lore, Mid-American Review, Agni*, and many others. In 2013, he recorded his translations of Dan Turèll, a Danish beatnik poet, to the background music of Halfdan E (an award-winning film composer) on *Dan Turèll+Halfdan E meets Thomas E. Kennedy* (PlantSounds Records).

Since 2004, he has taught fiction and creative nonfiction in the Fairleigh Dickinson University MFA Program and lives in Copenhagen.

BILL PERSKY is a five-time Emmy Award-winning writer, director, and producer for such shows as *The Dick Van Dyke Show, That Girl*, Sid Caesar's *Your Show of Shows* and *The Sid Caesar, Imogene Coca, Carl Reiner, Howard Morris Special, The Bill Cosby Special*, and *Kate and Allie*.

After a start at WNEW radio in New York in the mid 1950s, he moved to California to write for a variety of shows including *The Steve Allen Show, The Andy Williams Show, The Julie Andrews Show, McHale's Navy*, and *The Joey Bishop Show*, until he found a home with Carl Reiner on *The Dick Van Dyke Show*. After three years as a writer, story editor, and two Emmys, Bill and his partner, Sam Denoff, followed by creating the Emmy-nominated *That Girl*, for Marlo Thomas.

In the mid 1970s, the successful partnership ended amicably, as Persky turned to directing, specializing in TV pilots. From 1975-1982 he directed 22 pilots, of which 16 were put on the air as series, the most memorable being *Who's the Boss?*.

There were also five television films, and the Paramount feature, *Serial*, before he moved back to New York to produce and direct 100 episodes of the series, *Kate and Allie*, winning an Emmy for directing.

Of late, he has compiled a memoir of stories, both professional and personal, which he performs as a one-man show, *Whisper Whoopie*, and is a contributing writer to *USA Today*.

He is also a guest lecturer at NYU Film School and Yale University, and teaches comedy writing at The New York Film Academy

NICHOLAS PILEGGI began his writing career as a journalist for Associated Press in the 1950s specializing in crime reporting. Over the next 30 years he built up his contacts and reputation, covering stories for *New York* magazine and contributing to many others, as he became an expert on crime, most especially the organized crime world of the Mafia.

In 1986 he wrote *Wiseguy* which he subsequently developed into the Academy Award-winning screenplay for *Goodfellas* (1990) with Martin Scorsese. He followed that with scripts for *Casino* (1995) (also based on one of his books, and also developed with Scorsese), and *City*

Hall (1996), as well as writing and producing several other crime-based movies and TV shows.

ADAM PLANTINGA holds a B.A. in English with a second major in criminology/law studies from Marquette University, where he graduated Phi Beta Kappa and magna cum laude in 1995. Plantinga's short story "Untitled" was included in the anthology, *25 and Under: Fiction*, and *Washington Post* book critic George Garrett called it his candidate for the best story in the book. He has written thirteen nonfiction articles on various aspects of police work for the literary magazine *The Cresset*, published by the Valparaiso University Press. Plantinga was a City of Milwaukee police officer from 2001 to 2008, including time spent as a field training officer. He is currently a sergeant with the San Francisco Police Department. He lives in the Bay Area with his wife and daughters. *400 Things Cops Know* is his first book.

DAVID L. ROBBINS graduated with a B.A. in Theater and Speech from the College of William & Mary in Williamsburg, Virginia. Having little actual theatrical talent, he didn't know what to do for a living. Robbins decided to attend what he calls the "great catch-basin of unfocused over-achievers": law school. He received his Juris Doctorate at William and Mary in 1980, then practiced environmental law in Columbia, S.C. for precisely a year. Robbins decided to attend Psychology school, but while waiting for admisison in 1981, he began a successful freelance writing career. He began writing fiction in 1990, and has since published twelve novels including several bestsellers. He is currently working on the thirteenth, as well as several scripts for the stage and screen.

Robbins is the co-founder of the James River Writers, a non-profit group in his hometown of Richmond that helps aspiring writers and students work and learn together as a writing community. He also co-founded The Podium Foundation, a non-profit which brings writing and critical reasoning programs to the students of Richmond's city high schools. He also teaches advanced creative writing as a visiting professor at Virginia Commonwealth University's Honors College.

STEVE SZILAGYI, critic, journalist, and novelist, graduated with honors from Columbia University, winning the Columbia Bennett Cerf Award for Fiction for his unpublished story collection, *The Night Sophia Loren's Dress Caught Fire in a Restaurant,* as well as the Pushcart Prize for Outstanding Writer. *Photographing Fairies* was short-listed for the 1993 World Fantasy Award, and was made into a 1996 movie starring Ben Kingsley, and directed by Nick Willing. He is also co-author of *The Advocate* (2000), which took top honors in the novel-writing category of The Writers Foundation's annual America's Best competition.

Also a painter and illustrator, Szilagyi has published drawings in *New York Magazine* and other national publications.

He is the winner of a Cleveland Emmy Award (1996), and First Place winner for Best Arts Writing, Ohio Society of Professional Journalists awards (2001).

SUZANNE TRAUTH has co-authored *Sonia Moore and American Acting Training,* and co-edited *Katrina on Stage: Five Plays* (Northwestern University Press). Her novels include *Souvenirs* and *Show Time,* (Kensington Books, 2016). For TheatreFest, she directed, served as Associate Producer, and founded the experimental Next Stage. She co-produced and directed productions at the Ensemble Studio Theatre (NYC), the Whole Theatre, and 12 Miles West. Ms. Trauth served as Assistant Artistic Director and faculty member at the Sonia Moore Studio in NYC and performed for the American Stanislavski Theatre. As part of a global initiative, she directed *The Crucible* for the Theatre-on-Podol in the Ukraine. She is a former member of the theatre faculty at Montclair State University in Montclair, N.J. where she coordinated the BFA Acting Program, and is a member of the Dramatists Guild

Ms. Trauth's plays include *Françoise,* which received staged readings at Luna Stage, West Orange, NJ, and Nora's Playhouse in Brooklyn, NY, was a Finalist in the Boomerang First Flight Festival, and recently nominated for the Kilroy List; *Midwives* developed at Playwrights Theatre of New Jersey; *Rehearsing Desire*; *iDream,* supported by the National Science Foundation's STEM initiative on science and technology and presented at Premiere Stages; and *Katrina: the K Word,* based on interviews with New Orleans' survivors of Hurricane Katrina, and produced on university campuses throughout the U.S. Ms. Trauth also directed a staged reading of *Katrina: the K Word* at Playwrights Theatre of New Jersey. Her screenplays *Solitaire* and *Boomer Broads* have won awards at the Austin Film Festival and the Writer's Network Competition, and, most recently, she wrote and directed the short film *Jigsaw*, nominated for best film in the shorts category at the PF3 Film Festival and screened at New Filmmakers, N.Y. She is currently a member of Playwrights Theatre of New Jersey Emerging Women Playwrights program.

ADRIANA TRIGIANI is beloved by millions of readers around the world for sixteen bestsellers, including the blockbuster epic *The Shoemaker's Wife*; the Big Stone Gap series; *Lucia, Lucia*; the Valentine series; the Viola series for young adults; and the bestselling memoir *Don't Sing at the Table*. Trigiani reaches new heights with *All the Stars in the Heavens*, an epic tale from the golden age of Hollywood. She is the award-winning filmmaker of the documentary *Queens of the Big Time*. Trigiani wrote and directed the major motion picture *Big Stone Gap*, based on her debut novel and filmed entirely on location in her Virginia hometown, released nationwide on October 9, 2015.

STEPHEN WHITTY has been writing about film for more than 30 years. A graduate of NYU's Tisch School of the Arts, his essays, reviews, interviews and short fiction have been published in America and abroad, and appeared in *Entertainment Weekly*, *Cosmopolitan*, and a variety of newspapers and websites. He is a two-time chair of the New York Film Critics Circle.

ARIEL S. WINTER, a long-time bookseller at The Corner Bookstore in New York City and Borders in Baltimore, is also the author of the children's picture book *One of a Kind*, and of the blog We Too Were Children, Mr. Barrie, devoted to the rediscovery of long-forgotten children's books written by literary icons such as John Updike, Langston Hughes, and Gertrude Stein. His writing has appeared in *The*

Urbanite and on *McSweeney's Internet Tendency*, and in 2008 he won the Free Press "Who Can Save Us Now?" short story contest.

REFERENCED WORKS

Beneath the Neon Egg, Thomas E. Kennedy. Bloomsbury, 2014.

Chinaman's Chance, Ross Thomas. Minotaur Books 2004 reprint of 1978 original.

The Cocktail Waitress, James M. Cain. Hard Case Crime, 2013.

Death in the Afternoon, Ernest Hemingway. Scribner's 1996 reprint of 1932 original.

400 Things Cops Know: Street-Smart Lessons from a Veteran Patrolman, Adam Plantinga. Quill Driver Books, 2014.

The Friends of Eddie Coyle, George V. Higgins. Picador 2010 reprint of 1972 original.

House of Psychotic Women: An Autobiographical Topography of Female Neurosis in Horror and Exploitation Films, Kier-La Janisse. FAB Press, 2012.

In Search of Lost Time (aka *Remembrance of Things Past): Swann's Way*. Marcel Proust. Amazon Digital Services 2012 reprint of 1922 Charles Kenneth Scott-Moncrieff translation .

"The Lagoon," Joseph Conrad. Reprinted in *"The Lagoon" and Other Stories*, Oxford University Press, 1998.

The Maltese Falcon, Warner Bros. 1941, writer/director John Huston, adapted from the Dashiell Hammet novel.

My Life Is a Situation Comedy, Bill Persky. Mandevilla Press, 2012.

The Peacemakers, Richard Herman. Richard Herman, 2012.

Photographing Fairies, Steve Szilagyi. Ballantine, 1992.

Point Blank, Sonny Grosso and Philip Rosenberg. Avon, 1979.

The Shoemaker's Wife, Adriana Trigiani. Harper, 2012.

The 20-Year Death, Ariel S. Winter. Hard Case Crime, 2012.

War of the Rats, David L. Robbins. Bantam, 2000.

The Waves, Virginia Woolf. Harcourt 2006 reprint of 1931 original.

World and Town, Gish Jen. Knopf, 2010.

Excerpts from Adam Plantinga's *400 Things Cops Know* are reprinted with the permission of Quill Driver Books.

Excerpts from Kier-La Janisse's *House of Psychotic Women: An Autobiographical Topography of Female Neurosis in Horror and Exploitation Films* are reprinted with the permission of FAB Press.

Excerpts from Gish Jen's *World and Town* are reprinted with the permission of Penguin Random House.

Excerpts from *My Life Is a Situation Comedy*, *The Peacemakers*, *Photographing Fairies*, and *Point Blank* are reprinted with the permission of the authors.

ACKNOWLEDGMENTS

A great, great thanks to the contributors to these essays; people who, without exception, were wonderfully generous with their time, their accessibility, and their willingness to share their thoughts and observations. Class acts all.

Another tremendous thanks goes to the Creative Writing MFA program at Fairleigh Dickinson under the guidance of Rene Steinke. This book was a direct result of my time there, and any positive qualities it has are a product of the high caliber of the program and its faculty.

I feel compelled to single out those people – both mentors and my peers – who made my time in the program a memorable chapter for me both professionally and personally. So, special thanks to The Walter & Ellen Show – my editor, Walter Cummins, and Ellen Akins; Renee Ashley, who did what I thought for years was impossible – got me to understand poetry; the dog whisperer, Jean LoPorto; one of the most sensitive souls I've ever known, Trevor Payne; the Big Fisherman, Rogan Kelly; and my favorite roomie, Jeff Vashista.

And, of course and as always, my family who puts up with a lot from me. I mean, a *lot*.

"What Do You Mean You *Can't* Do It?" originally appeared in edited form as, "Tell, Don't Show: Parts One and Two" on *KYSO Flash*, issue #3, spring 2015.

"War Among the Ruins: David L. Robbins and *War of the Rats*" originally appeared under the title, "A Book Review Interview: David L. Robbins and Historical Fiction," in *New Letters*, December 2015 issue.

"The Case of the Disappearing Private Eye: An Interview with Ariel S. Winter" originally appeared as part of a larger piece on *Sound on Sight*, August 10, 2012.

"Raising Cain: Charles Ardai on James M. Cain's *The Cocktail Waitress*" originally appeared as, "Raising Cain: The Work of James M. Cain," on *Sound on Sight*, Septembmer 18, 2012.

"A Life Reflected in Art; the Art Reflected in a Life: Kier-La Janisse and *House of Psychotic Women*" originally appeared in *Serving House Journal*, November 2015 issue.

"Cop's Eyes: Adam Plantinga and *400 Things Cops Know*" originally appeared as "Cop's Eyes: Adam Plantinga's debut book *400 Things Cops Know: Street-Smart Lessons from a Veteran Patrolman*" in *New Letters*, Winter 2015 issue.

"Preserving an Icon: Max Allan Collins on Mickey Spillane" originally appeared as "Max Allan Collins *(Road to Perdition)* on Carrying on Mickey Spillane's Legacy" on *Sound on Sight*, May 17, 2012.

"Black and Blue: Thomas E. Kennedy and His Non-*Noir Noir, Beneath the Neon Egg*" originally appeared in *New Letters*, January 2015 issue.

"A Writer's Reboot" originally appeared as "Writer's Boot Camp" on *The Write Place at the Write Time*, winter/spring issue 2014.

Bill Mesce, Jr. is a writer and college instructor living in New Jersey. His most recent work includes the WW II novel *A Cold and Distant Place*, and the nonfiction book, *Inside the Rise of HBO: A Personal History of the Company That Transformed Television* and *Idols, Icons, and Illusions: The Movies We Love – and Love to Hate – and the People Who Made Them*.